SPECIAL MESSAGE TO READERS

This book is published by

THE ULVERSCROFT FOUNDATION

a registered charity in the U.K., No. 264873

The Foundation was established in 1974 to provide funds to help towards research, diagnosis and treatment of eye diseases. Below are a few examples of contributions made by THE ULVERSCROFT FOUNDATION:

A new Children's Assessment Unit at Moorfield's Hospital, London.

•

Twin operating theatres at the Western Ophthalmic Hospital, London.

•

The Frederick Thorpe Ulverscroft Chair of Ophthalmology at the University of Leicester.

•

Eye Laser equipment to various eye hospitals.

If you would like to help further the work of the Foundation by making a donation or leaving a legacy, every contribution, no matter how small, is received with gratitude. Please write for details to:

THE ULVERSCROFT FOUNDATION,
The Green, Bradgate Road, Anstey,
Leicester LE7 7FU. England
Telephone: (0533) 364325

GUNSIGHT

He turned the streets of Gunsight into bloody avenues of war . . . He was marshal of Gunsight. He was also Jim Parker, desperate outlaw-killer . . . most hunted man in the whole bullet-torn southwest.

Books by Frank Gruber
in the Linford Western Library:

BROKEN LANCE
LONESOME RIVER

1

THE cowboys had been drunk when they boarded the train, and the moment they were seated they proceeded to improve their condition. They passed a bottle around until it was empty and then one of them casually threw it out of the window. The window happened to be closed at the time.

The conductor was taking tickets in the car when the glass crashed. His mouth tight, he walked forward to remonstrate with the drunken cowboys. Jill Layton couldn't hear what the conductor said, but she heard the reply of one of the cowboys. She also saw him whip out a long-barreled revolver and thrust it at the conductor's feet.

"Dance, you ticket-punchin' yellow-belly!" the cowboy snarled. "Dance, or I'll shoot off your toes."

The conductor's voice rose hysterically.

"Please, gentlemen, you're frightening the passengers . . . "

"I said dance!" roared the cowboy with the revolver. He fired a bullet into the floor less than an inch from the conductor's foot.

The latter tried to leap back, but one of the cowboy's cronies caught him. "Mose said to dance and he means it, mister."

Directly ahead of Jill a tall, slender man got up and began to walk forward. A sudden feeling of impending disaster swept over Jill. The man was going to interfere . . . and there were five of the drunken cowboys. And the man . . . why, he was no more than a boy, perhaps not even more than Jill's twenty. She had a glimpse of his lean, clean-shaven face and then he was behind the conductor.

He said in a clear voice, "Put away your gun and keep quiet. Or get off this train!"

The drunken men began turning and a revolver appeared – out of nowhere, it seemed to Jill – in the youth's hand. His hand whipped forward and up and the barrel of the gun smacked against the threatening cowboy's head.

The man crumpled to the floor of the train, like a sack of wheat. The youth's revolver made a swift sidewards movement and the muzzle stopped against the stomach of the man who had caught the conductor from the rear.

The youth didn't say a word. He merely kept the gun pressed against the man and looked at his companions. It was one of the latter who spoke first.

"We was only havin' a little fun."

"Have it somewhere else," the lean young man said, then. "Somewhere out on the prairie . . . Conductor, stop the train."

The conductor turned a look of awe on the young man. Then, without a word, he reached up and pulled the cord.

The train began stopping so suddenly that Jill Layton was thrown violently against the seat ahead. When she had recovered herself, she looked quickly forward again. The young man was still in command of the situation. And as the train came to a full halt, he supervised the dismounting of the drunks. Two of them dragged their unconscious companion with them.

In a moment the train was starting and then the youth turned and began walking back to his seat. His long-barreled revolver had disappeared.

Jill, in common with the other passengers, studied him. He was a full six feet tall, but weighed no more than a hundred and sixty. The black Prince Albert he wore made him look even thinner. His eyes looked neither to the right nor the left, but as he came to his seat they suddenly met Jill's own eyes. Just for an instant, but in that moment it seemed to Jill that he looked right through her. They were pale blue, piercing eyes.

At close range, his face was still youthful, but there was something taut and strained about it that indicated he was older than Jill had thought at first . . . But not much older.

He sat down in his seat by the window,

leaned his head back and pulled his black felt hat down over his eyes. For all Jill knew, he went instantly to sleep.

The conductor came along after a moment and, leaning toward his rescuer, said, "That was right nervy of you, stranger. And I'm mighty thankful."

The tall young man made no reply. He did not even signify that he heard the conductor and, after a moment, the latter moved away.

Jill tried to look at the Kansas landscape that was flitting by outside the train window, but her eyes kept returning to the back of the young man's head. He never stirred, not even when the train stopped an hour later and the conductor announced that there would be a half-hour's stop for dinner.

Jill got up and left the train. On the station platform she paused to regard the "town." It consisted of a half-dozen ramshackle buildings and an unpainted station, which contained a lunch counter.

Jill seated herself and ordered food. She was cutting off a piece of tough fried steak when the young man of the train suddenly seated himself beside her and said, "I certainly hope Uncle Ben got our telegram and meets us at the train."

Jill stared at him, "I beg your pardon?"

"Smile," he said, "and talk. And don't look around. . . . If Uncle Ben doesn't meet us at the train, we'll put up at a hotel. But you know what those trail town hotels are like."

"I won't mind," Jill said, quickly. "It won't be the Planter's Hotel in St. Louis, but we can stand it for a night." She smiled, hesitated a moment, then placed her hand on his arm.

He looked at her warmly. "I wasn't hungry, but I guess I'll have something to eat after all."

"It'll do you good," Jill said. "Waiter, bring my . . ." she hesitated just a fraction, "bring my husband a steak. Medium rare . . ."

And then the man beside Jill leaped back off the lunch counter stool. His face was taut and in his eyes was the same expression with which he had regarded Jill on the train. He said, simply: "Thanks!" then sprang for the door.

At the far end of the lunch counter a heavy-set man with an enormous walrus mustache cried out: "Here, stop, you!"

But the lean man did not stop. He jerked open the door of the lunch room and stepped through. The mustached man began swearing as he rushed for the door. As he came abreast, Jill suddenly got up from her stool. The big man collided squarely with her and would have knocked her off her feet, but that Jill threw herself toward the door. She clutched it desperately, clung to it as the big man wrestled her away.

Jill delayed him perhaps five seconds altogether. But then he was outside and almost instantly Jill heard the dull boom of a revolver.

By the time Jill got out on the station platform the heavy-set man was running toward the hitch-rail of a saloon. The lean young man was already astride a sleek sorrel that he had evidently commandeered.

The mustached man stopped in the middle of the street, took careful aim and emptied his revolver. The shots produced no visible results, for the horseman leaned far forward in the saddle and offered very little target.

The train passengers were pouring out of the station restaurant when the big man turned back. Jill saw the grim look on his face and, suddenly frightened, turned to the train.

"Wait a minute, miss!"

Jill stopped. A cold wind seemed to blow upon her spine. But she raised her head proudly.

"Were you addressing me?" she asked, haughtily.

"I was," the big man said, grimly. "Do you know that you helped that man escape?"

"Escape? What do you mean?"

"I would have got him if you hadn't helped him by blocking the door in there. I had him dead to rights."

Jill's nostrils flared. "I don't know

what you're talking about. But I do know that you're about the rudest man I've ever met. You practically knocked me down and then you accuse me of . . ."

"Whoa, lady!" the mustached man said, angrily. "I happen to be a detective and that man you prevented me from capturing is a dangerous criminal. And you know what I think? I think you're his accomplice . . ."

"Accomplice?" cried Jill. "Why, how dare you? I barely knew the man. He happened to do something on the train that put us all under obligations to him and when he addressed me in the dining-room, I naturally answered him."

The train conductor had come forward. He bobbed his head up and down. "The lady's telling the truth. That man you claim is a criminal just happened to save my life on the train, that's all."

The detective whirled on the conductor. "What are you talking about? Do you know who that man was?"

"No," retorted the conductor, "but I'm thinking you're making a mistake about him."

"There's no mistake," said the detective. "That man was Jim Parker!"

"Jim Parker!" cried one or two of the train passengers.

"Jim Parker himself," said the detective. "My agency had word that he was on this train and they telegraphed me to head him off."

"You're with the Bligh Detective Agency?" someone asked.

The detective nodded. "I'm Captain Street."

Even Jill Layton had heard of Captain Street. He was the most famous detective in the country, after Colonel Bligh himself. The newspapers were filled with his exploits, for Colonel Bligh believed in publicity for his agency. Favorable publicity. He needed it, to offset the unfavorable that he had received in his long pursuit of Harvey Dawson. Dawson, the most notorious outlaw of the decade, who had laughed at the law of a dozen states. He had laughed the loudest and longest at Colonel Bligh, head of the international detective agency that bore his name.

Bligh had pursued Harvey Dawson long and hard, and his every effort had resulted in failure. Dawson was as free today as he had ever been. And so was every member of his gang. Only one, in fact, had ever been apprehended and that one had scarcely been incarcerated than he had made a daring jailbreak.

That man's name was Jim Parker.

And Jim Parker, according to Captain Street, was the lean, young man of the train, the youth who had rescued the conductor from the drunken cowboys. Yes, that man could be Jim Parker. Except that he was so young.

2

"DODGE CITY!" the conductor announced, and almost everyone in the train made preparations to get off. Among them was Jill Layton. She shivered a little, for even in St. Louis she had heard wild stories about Dodge City and her Aunt Maud had almost refused to permit her to make the trip.

"Your father hasn't any sense about such things," Aunt Maud had stormed. "Look what he did to Jennie, my poor sister, taking her down there to Arizona where there isn't anything but desert and savage Indians. And now he wants you to meet him in Dodge City!"

"But Aunt Maud," Jill had protested, "Dad wouldn't be asking me to meet him there if he didn't think it was all right. I don't believe it's as bad as the newspapers say it is. After all, we have cowboys down in Arizona and they're a pretty decent sort. They don't become killers the moment they get away from home."

So now she was getting off the train at Dodge City. The station platform was crowded with men, women and even children. There were a few cowboys present, too, but they looked respectable enough.

"Jill!" cried a hoarse voice.

Her father reached for her and Jill went into his arms. She caught a whiff of his breath as he kissed her and knew he had been drinking. Well, he took a drink at home once in a while. But otherwise he looked no different than at home. Except that he was better dressed.

He wore a suit of black broadcloth, with a brocaded vest and a soft white shirt. His trousers were tucked into a pair of brand-new, highly polished boots and he wore a new broad-brimmed hat.

He was glad to see Jill and he kept an arm about her as he led her from the platform. A colored man got Jill's luggage and followed with it.

Away from the station, Jill saw that they were walking down a wide street which had wooden buildings on both sides. Why, Dodge City looked just like any Middle Western town, say on a Saturday when the folks came in from the farms.

The hotel was a cool, pleasant establishment. The rooms were rather small, but nicely furnished. After she had washed and changed from her traveling dress, she joined her father in his own adjoining room.

He regarded her with a fond light in his eyes and shook his head. "Jill, you've grown up. You were a girl when I sent you to visit your Aunt Maud last year. Now, you're a woman, in so short a time."

"I'm nineteen, Father."

"So you are. You were only seven when we moved to Arizona."

"I can hardly wait to get back. Dad, Mother is all right?"

"Of course. She couldn't make the trip. I came overland, you know, with the herd. I thought my business would keep me here another ten days, but I couldn't wait to see you, so I had you come out. Now, I find, I'm just about ready to go. We'll take the train back to St. Louis, then the steamer to New Orleans and go from there by boat to Brownsville, Texas. It'll be an interesting trip."

"Of course, Dad, but you forget that I made it last year coming up."

"So you did. Jill, this will surprise you; I'm no longer in partnership with Andrew Spence . . ."

Jill exclaimed softly, "Dad, you haven't – "

"No, we're still friends. It's just – well, we haven't been seeing eye to eye about things the last couple of years. I'm getting along, you know, and Andrew's son, Kearney, is growing up . . . "

"How is he?"

"Kearney? He's here, in Dodge. Say . . . " George Layton looked sharply at his daughter. Then a cloud seemed to pass over his face. "It's hard for me to talk to you, Jill. You seem so grown up and I haven't seen you in a year."

"I haven't changed, Father," Jill said, steadily. "You were going to say – about Kearney Spence?"

"Kearney's twenty-one, Jill. He's – well, he's been doing a man's work. He brought up one of the herds and did a good job of it, too. I guess he's entitled to a little fun."

"You mean Kearney's drinking?"

George Layton shrugged. "No more so than the rest, I guess. He'll have plenty of time to settle down on the way home, because I understand he's going down the trail with the boys."

Kearney Spence was twenty-one. He had always been a bit wild. Yet his father had a strong hand and could hold him in, when he was at home. But suppose the hand of Andrew Spence wasn't there to steady Kearney, what would happen to him then?

Would Kearney become like some wild young men . . . Jim Parker, for example?

"Dad," Jill said suddenly, "have you

ever heard of Jim Parker?"

"Jim Parker? No, I don't know anyone by that name. There's an outlaw . . ."

"That's the one. He *is* an outlaw? A – a notorious one?"

"He's one of Harvey Dawson's men. But why should you ask about him?"

"I met him."

"What?" cried George Layton. "Where?"

"On the train. There were some drunken cowboys threatening the conductor. This Jim Parker made them leave the train. He stopped it and . . . he didn't look like an outlaw, Dad. I – " She blurted out the whole story, including her own part in it. When she finished, George Layton regarded her thoughtfully for a moment. Then he said, quietly:

"Make no mistake about it, Jill, Jim Parker *is* an outlaw. Harvey Dawson is one of the deadliest, most desperate men who ever lived. And anyone who rides with him is made of the same stuff. Perhaps I made a mistake asking you to come five hundred miles on the train by yourself. But it won't happen again.

Now suppose we go down and have some lunch?"

They left their rooms and started down the stairs. As they reached the little lobby, a man came hurriedly out of a door across the room. He forgot to close the door entirely and Jill heard a commotion inside the room. A man's voice cried out:

"I got money and it's good any damn place."

"Not here," a voice said, firmly. "You're drunk and if you want to drink and raise hell, go down below the railroad. They'll welcome you there."

The front door opened and a tall man with a walrus mustache came into the hotel and headed for the partly opened door. As he moved across the room he drew a long-barreled blue revolver.

George Layton caught hold of Jill's arm and moved her hurriedly to the front door. Jill went willingly enough, expecting any moment to hear the crash of gunfire inside the hotel. But it didn't materialize.

Layton led Jill across the street to the general store. As they entered, Jill shot a quick look around and saw the tall, walrus-mustached-man emerge from the hotel. He was stooping . . . because he was dragging an unconscious man by the coat collar.

Jill exclaimed softly, "Father, look – "

"I know," George Layton said, "I recognized his voice."

"What – what do you mean?" She was a bit mystified.

"The buffaloed man; it's Kearney Spence. Isn't that what you meant, Jill?"

"Oh, no, Dad! Kearney . . . is he hurt?"

"He'll have a splitting head tomorrow. Wyatt Earp – that's the marshal – has acquired a fine technique for buffaloing cowboys. He does it every day. Kearney had it coming to him, all right."

Jill shuddered. "But Dad, oughtn't we do something?"

"Andy Spence will take care of Kearney. He's here too, you know. Came to close our deal. I wonder how it'll work out, two cattle ranches in Gunsight Valley."

That, neither George Layton nor Jill was to know for a long time to come. It was days before they reached home. From Dodge City they had to take the train to St. Louis, where they spent a day with Aunt Maud. Then they engaged passage on a river steamer and floated down the Mississippi to New Orleans. They remained in the Creole city for three days, then embarked on another steamer which took them into the choppy Gulf of Mexico and in due course landed them at Brownsville, Texas.

There, George Layton learned some astonishing news. "Gunsight, Arizona?" the stagecoach agent exclaimed. "You'll have to wait three days. We're running two stages a day for Gunsight and they're full up until the second stage, three days from now. Just nothing to do but wait."

"Whoa!" cried Layton. "You're making a mistake. There aren't six people a month traveling to Gunsight." He laughed easily.

"It's *your* mistake, mister," the agent retorted. "They've had the biggest gold strike the Southwest's ever seen and every man and his cousin is headin' for Gunsight."

3

JIM PARKER heard of the strike in the Indian Nations, two hundred miles south of Dodge City. At first it made no impression on him. Then he reached the appallingly flat Texas Panhandle where a man could see fifty miles in each direction and he rode an entire day without being able to lose a speck that was behind him. When darkness fell he cut sharply to the west and rode until nearly dawn. He hobbled his horse then and slept for three hours.

When he awoke he saw a horseman only a few miles to the east and another farther away, in the north.

He debated waiting it out.

They might be just cowboys in which case there would be no harm. But — they might not be cowboys. He had come six hundred miles in two weeks and always there had been someone behind him. He had killed a horse and worn another, purchased from an Osage, to a frazzle and still someone remained on his trail.

He thought of Gunsight. There were mountains in Arizona, rough, wild mountains and fierce Apaches. Men did not travel alone in that country. Not unless they were desperate. Well, Jim Parker was desperate. The chase had been too long. He couldn't run forever.

Far in the west he could see the blue haze of a mountain range. There ought to be sanctuary in the mountains.

He headed for them. He rode all day and the mountains came no nearer. After dark he ate a cold supper and hobbled his horse. He rolled up in a blanket and was asleep almost instantly.

He slept for three hours, then got up and caught his mount and, saddling, rode due south for two hours, then another hour to the west, after which he again hobbled his horse and went to sleep.

He was up at sunrise and examined

his horse critically. It was in poor shape. It was probably good for two or three days more if not pushed too hard, but it needed a long rest and some grain, which Parker did not have.

The land today was a little more rolling than it had been the last few days and Parker was thankful for that. And because he saw no other horsemen. Toward noon he discovered that he was climbing slowly. The mountains did not seem as far away, nor as steep. He rested his horse for a couple of hours, then headed west again.

Late in the afternoon he saw a house, but gave it a wide berth. Just before dark he saw another and then, when darkness fell, he saw a cluster of lights in the far distance. He ate the last of his jerked meat and after a short rest for his mount rode on again.

It was near midnight when he rode into a small town and was told at the livery stable that it was called Roswell and was well into New Mexico territory. He put the horse up at the stable, paying for a good feed of grain, then walked out of the town a half-mile and went to sleep in the open.

In the morning he went to the livery stable and discovered that his horse was in no condition to travel. "What she needs is 'bout a week of rest and grain feedin'," the liveryman told him. "You must've come pretty fast with her." He screwed up his mouth. "Headin' for Lincoln?"

"Lincoln?" asked Parker. "Where's that?"

"Down here a ways."

"South?"

"And west. Busy place these days."

"Gold?"

"Not that." The liveryman looked at him shrewdly. "Me, I'm neutral, but I hear that a good man can draw good wages there."

Parker shook his head. "Is Lincoln on the road to Gunsight?"

"Gunsight, ah! Should have known, but you looked more like – "

"Like what?"

"Never mind. I talk too much. Yep, Lincoln's on the way to Gunsight, but you got a spell of travelin' after Lincoln and the Apaches are out. You're all right as long as you're in the Ruidoso, but after that you've got the White Sands, then Las Cruces and a long jump to Lordsburg and then some more to Bisbee and Gunsight. You're goin' there the hard way."

"Then I'll need a good horse. That black gelding over there . . . is it your own horse?"

"Yep, but he ain't for sale. Best horse I've ever owned in my life and no money could buy him."

"My jaded horse and a hundred and fifty dollars."

The liveryman blinked. "Mister, that's a lot of money, but . . ."

"Two hundred."

The horseman groaned. "I don't make two hundred dollars in three months."

"I need a good horse. Three hundred."

The liveryman threw up his hands. "All right, on one condition, that you keep travelin' west."

"I aim to, but why?"

"Because the title ain't so good east of the line. I bought the horse from a man who was comin' through pretty fast."

Parker thought for a moment, then went over to examine the gelding closely and was lost. "It's a deal," he said.

At a combination general store and saloon he bought some food for himself and twenty-five pounds of ear corn. Then he headed out of town, along a well-beaten road leading up into the mountains. Soon he was riding past piñon trees and by mid-afternoon was cool enough to be comfortable. The trees were taller.

He met a couple of riders coming north. They were shifty-eyed men and carried rifles as well as pistols. They barely nodded as they rode past Parker.

An hour before sunset Parker saw the most astonishing thing he had seen since he had left Kansas, a double row of trees forming a lane that led a quarter of a mile to a magnificent house. The house would have been a show place in a Kansas City suburb; here it was incredible.

He sat on his black gelding and stared down the lane of planted trees. Finally he shook his head and turned the gelding. At that moment a man rose from the ground behind one of the trees. There was a rifle in his hand, that was pointed carelessly at Parker.

"Howdy, stranger," he said.

Parker doubted if the man could get him with the rifle but a shot would bring men from the house and Parker was not inclined to flight and a long chase. He said, easily,

"Howdy; is this the road to Lincoln?"

"That depends; who was you plannin' to see in Lincoln?"

"No one in particular. I'm a stranger in these parts."

"Texas?"

Parker shook his head. "Further."

"Then I think you better come have a talk with the boss. As long as you aren't a Texas man you'll want to work on the right side."

Parker shrugged. "I'll talk to the boss, anyway."

The rifleman fell in beside and a little to the rear. As they neared the big house, the odor of barbecued beef assailed Parker's nostrils, and he glanced to the right and saw a crowd of men in a small grove of cottonwoods. A couple of the men were turning a side of beef on a spit over a fire.

A sandy-haired youth with slightly protruding teeth disengaged himself from the group and came toward Parker. The latter dismounted.

"Howdy," he said, "I'm lookin' for the boss."

"He's from up north," said the rifleman behind Parker.

The buck-tooth youth grinned. "How far north?"

"Quite a ways. Mind pointing out the boss?"

The boy couldn't have been more than eighteen or nineteen. He shook his head. "How far north? Kansas?"

"Maybe."

"My name's Bonney," said the boy. "I'm ramroddin' for John Chisum . . . practically. You wouldn't be from Missouri?"

Parker looked thoughtfully at young Bonney. "Why?"

"I just thought maybe. Say, come over here where we can talk."

Bonney walked out of earshot of the other cowboys. Parker followed leisurely, walking in a half-circle so he could still see the other men. Bonney seemed to make thoughtful note of that. When Parker came up, he said:

"You never heard my name? Billy Bonney?"

"Sorry; should I have?"

Bonney seemed disappointed. "I guess not . . . up in Missouri. Look, you wouldn't happen to know any of the boys?"

"I know some Missouri people, yes. But it's a big state."

"You know what I mean, stranger. You're ridin' a good horse and you're goin' to Lincoln. Ever hear of Harvey Dawson?"

"The outlaw? Is he here?"

Bonney exclaimed, "Cut it out. What's your name?"

"Smith."

"Smith of Missouri," jeered young Bonney. "Yah!"

"I'll be riding along," Parker said, coldly.

"No, you won't, just yet. Tom! Tom O'Pholiard!"

A tall, slim man in his early twenties came up. "Tom," said Bonney. "Tell this stranger who I am."

O'Pholiard grinned. "Billy Bonney; Billy the Kid."

"He never heard of me, Tom. Look, remember that newspaper I was readin' last week, about those Missouri boys? What was the name of that fellow who made a monkey of Cap Street out in Kansas?"

"Jim Parker!" exclaimed O'Pholiard. His eyes went to Parker.

"Yeah," said Billy Bonney. "Remember the description, about six feet, maybe twenty-four, slender . . . Murphy send for you, Parker?"

"I don't know anyone named Murphy," Parker replied, deliberately.

"It's just as well you don't," Bonney snapped, "because I aim to kill him one of these days. You'd better come work with us, Parker."

"I'm not sticking around. I'm going to Gunsight."

"Gunsight? Say! Yeah, I get it. They've had a big gold strike there. Mmm, every man to his game, I guess, but I didn't think Harvey Dawson ever worked that far south."

"You're pretty sure of things, aren't you, Bonney?"

"Pretty sure. I know a bullet's going to get me one of these days, but before it does, well, I'll leave my mark in these hills. Yeah, Gunsight; it sounds good, but I don't feel it. My bullet's around here. I dunno. Maybe yours is waiting for you in Gunsight, Jim Parker of Missouri!"

Jim Parker looked to the south and west. "Maybe it is, Billy the Kid."

4

PARKER had his first brush with the Apaches shortly after crossing the appalling stretch of the White Sands. The black gelding justified the price Parker had paid for it, but it received a bullet in its left flank that didn't heal, and between Lordsburg and Bisbee the animal went lame.

Parker walked with the gelding for a while, but it became steadily worse. He nursed it along, walking and finally even carrying the saddle, but still the gelding collapsed.

He stood over the horse for some minutes after he pulled back the hammer of his rifle. But finally he fired.

He left his saddle by the horse. He had miles and miles of desert travel ahead of him. Apaches might be concealed behind any boulder or rush out of any gulch. After a half-hour he came to a well defined and traveled road, leading west and south. He followed it and toward midday, when the sun was at its hottest, he finally heard behind him the drumming of horses' hoofs.

Looking back, he saw first of all an enormous cloud of dust, then after a few minutes a stagecoach, coming at a dead run pulled by six horses.

When the coach was still a hundred yards away he held up his hand. The horses did not slacken speed until they were within fifty feet. Parker stepped to the side of the road and the coach thundered past him. It continued a short distance beyond before the driver began braking and pulling up his horses.

Parker ran up behind it. As he approached he discovered that he was being covered by a shotgun in the hands of a man riding on top with his legs hanging over the boot and by a Sharps rifle in the grip of a man standing up beside the driver.

"Who're you?" cried the man with the shotgun.

"Just a traveler," Parker replied. "My horse was wounded by Indians and passed out. Can I buy passage to Gunsight?"

The driver, who was still fighting his spirited horses, managed to get up and yell over his shoulder. "You can, if you give up your guns."

"Why?" Parker asked sharply.

"Road agents. We don't trust anyone here. Ain't goin' to take any chances you bein' in cahoots with a gang that'll stop us next bend we come to."

Parker debated the matter a moment, then nodded acquiescence. He handed his rifle to the guard riding over the boot, then drew his Frontier Mode and passed it up. "Where'll I ride?" he asked.

"Inside; there's room for just one more, if you squeeze. We lose a couple at Bisbee."

A man stuck his head out of the window of the door. "You couldn't get a skeleton in here."

"G'wan," cried the driver. "Squeeze!"

The door was opened reluctantly, and

Parker started to climb in, amid much squirming and shifting of passengers. A space of about six inches was finally made for him. He started to sit down and a female passenger exclaimed and drew away. Parker sat down on the edge of the seat, biting his lips.

The stagecoach was already rolling. Then Parker looked up . . . at Jill Layton. Her eyes were on his face; they were wide and a bit startled, but otherwise she showed no signs of recognition.

Parker stared at her for a long moment. He knew her; even though it was a month and a thousand miles back, he knew her.

He dropped his eyes.

A passenger said, "How much farther is it to Gunsight?"

A heavy-set man beside Jill Layton replied. "Not more than a half-hour to Bisbee, then three hours to Gunsight."

The woman next to Parker – he could smell her strong perfume – exclaimed: "Thank goodness! This isn't my idea of traveling. If they have to have gold strikes, why can't they have them in civilized country?"

A fat man wheezed: "You said it, miss. I been afraid for the last three days that them Apaches was goin' to attack us. . . . You say you had a fight with them, stranger."

The fat man was looking at Parker. "It wasn't a fight," Parker said. "They ambushed me and I ran. Fortunately, I had a swift horse."

"Yeah," said the fat man. "But them Apaches might be following us. Or signalling ahead . . . "

Outside a rifle whanged.

Above the passengers on the seat of the stage, a man cried out in agony. The rifle whanged again and the sound was punctuated by the roar of a shotgun. And then a body pitched past the door of the stage. At the same time the passengers were thrown together in a huddle as the stage was violently braked.

By the time they could untangle themselves, the stage had stopped. A face wearing a black mask appeared suddenly at the window and a hoarse voice cried: "Outside, everybody, and first man tries something gets lead!"

For just a moment there was stunned silence in the coach. Then the voice of the stage driver came down: "Better do as he says, folks!"

The masked man jerked open the door. The fat passenger was closest to it and almost fell out. The other passengers dismounted more decorously. Parker, looking at Jill Layton, saw her eyes filled with horror, staring at him.

Half rising from the seat, he froze.

"All right in there," snarled the masked man. He thrust his revolver into the interior of the coach, under Jill Layton's very chin. A shudder seemed to run through her and she climbed out of the coach.

Parker was the last one out. By then the other passengers were already lined up beside the coach. There were only two highwaymen in sight, the one who had compelled the passengers to alight and another, also masked, who stood ahead of the coach and to one side with a revolver in each hand.

The shotgun messenger who had been riding the boot was gone. His huddled body lay back on the road. The driver and the man beside him were standing up on their perch, hands raised in the air.

As Parker took his place in the line-up the bandit in front of the line stepped around and began relieving the passengers of their weapons. He took off his hat, revealing a shock of blond hair.

"All right," he snapped. "Put your contributions in this and damn the man who holds out, because I'm going to search you all when I get through."

George Layton was at the far end of the line. He dropped a thick wallet into the bandit's hat, saying through his teeth:

"This is the sorriest thing you've ever done. I'm George Layton."

"Yeah," sneered the bandit, "and I'm Harvey Dawson."

"I own a quarter of a million acres of land," said Layton. "I have a hundred men working for me. They'll – "

"They won't keep you from going to heaven, if you don't shut your trap pronto!"

"Father," exclaimed Jill Layton, "please . . . "

"Ah, your daughter!" The highwayman skipped the other passengers and came down to face Jill Layton. He smacked his lips. "A beauty, too! How 'bout a kiss?"

"Here's *my* money," said Jim Parker. He reached for his inside coat pocket. But his fingers were diverted before entering the pocket. They dipped down into his vest and came up with a short .41 double-barreled derringer.

The bandit was whirling on Parker as the latter thrust the derringer forward. It exploded less than two feet from the mask and the force of the bullet jerked the man back.

Parker took two quick steps forward, one sidewards . . . and stabbed the little derringer toward the second bandit, more than fifty feet away. The powerful little gun exploded a fraction before the bandit's gun, enough sooner to spoil the man's aim.

The bandit cried out, staggered and turned to run. Parker exclaimed under his breath. The little gun was a short-range weapon. He had wounded the second bandit, but not seriously. And he had no more bullets. He turned to scoop up one of the revolvers the first bandit had taken from the passengers, but there was such a scramble for the guns that no one got one for many seconds. Then everyone began banging away – at nothing!

The bandit had disappeared. The side of the rutted trail that was a road was lined with huge boulders. Evidently he had disappeared behind one and was making his way to where his horse was undoubtedly waiting for him.

The stage driver and remaining messenger vaulted to the ground and added to the confusion. By the time Jim Parker finally found his own Frontier Model, the mask had been stripped off the first bandit and it was discovered that Parker's derringer slug had torn the roof off the man's head.

Parker, moving away, suddenly came face to face with Jill Layton. She was regarding him steadily, her eyes wide. But there was no longer horror in them.

Someone clapped Parker on the shoulder. "Mister, that was the nerviest thing I ever saw in my life!"

The perfumed woman suddenly gave a screech and, throwing her arms about Parker's neck, tried to kiss him. He averted his face and took the kiss on his neck.

The others crowded around. George Layton slapped the fat wallet he had retrieved against his thigh. "You're going to Gunsight, stranger? Good! I want to have a talk with you there."

Parker nodded, frowning. "I think we'd better be going. You can't tell . . . "

"There may be more of them!" someone cried.

That did it. The passengers scrambled

for the stagecoach. It was the driver and the messenger who finally lifted the dead bandit and guard to the boot and lashed them there. Parker remained on the ground and when they had finished looked up inquiringly. "All right to ride with you?"

"Sure, sure!" cried the driver. "And here's your rifle. Lord, if you hadn't been along . . . !"

There was ample room for three men on the driver's seat, and Bisbee was reached inside of a half hour. There, the body of the bandit created a sensation. But the stage was overdue and the agent insisted it leave for Gunsight at once and try to make up on its schedule. Fresh horses were swiftly harnessed to the coach and inside of ten minutes after entering Bisbee, the coach was climbing the tortuous canyon along which Bisbee was laid out.

Beyond Bisbee the country was incredibly bleak and wild. The stagecoach careened around hairpin turns and at times seemed to be running up the very mountain itself.

But at last, when the sun was sinking in the west, the stagecoach made a last turn and rushed down upon the town of Gunsight. Parker whistled softly at his first sight of it. It was a town of tents, frame shacks and mud houses with here and there a false-fronted, two-story building.

The founders of the town had somehow managed to preserve a fairly wide stretch down the center for a street, but on each side of the street buildings had been erected seemingly without rhyme or reason. A fresh-lumber frame shack was flanked by a tent on one side, a mud-chinked Indian hogan on the other and in the rear perhaps a dugout.

The wide street was lined with horses at the hitch rails, wagons parked here and there and a welter of humanity crowding along the dirt sidewalks or dashing aimlessly along the street.

The stagecoach was halted before a red adobe shack, which had a wooden roof. Jim Parker was the first person off the coach, and by the time the passengers were piling out he had darted into a building next door, which turned out to be a saloon. So he missed seeing Jill Layton.

5

GUNSIGHT was a stunning shock to both George and Jill Layton. When they had left it, it had been a sleepy hamlet of a dozen buildings existing mainly because of the Layton-Spence ranch, which spread out in all directions, running down to the Mexican border and comprising close to a million acres of land. The population of the hamlet had been about thirty souls.

Now, it contained thousands of people. There were prospectors and prostitutes, laborers and leeches, miners and ministers, gamblers and gunmen. The magic word, gold, had brought them all to Gunsight.

George Layton helped Jill down from the stagecoach, then gaped in astonishment at the town of Gunsight. He was shaking his head and muttering, when a man wearing patched levis stepped out of the express office and spoke to him.

"This is home, boss!"

"Arch Cummings!" cried Layton. "Lord, what's happened here?"

Cummings shrugged. "They found gold. Howdy Miss Jill! You're lookin' growed up. Mighty purty."

"Why, thank you, Arch," said Jill Layton. "I left here a year ago to go to the city and now the city's come here. Rather colorful, isn't it?"

"You might call it that, miss," said Arch Cummings. "Me, I don't."

"You don't like it, Arch?"

"Two men was killed here today," said Arch Cummings, bluntly. "They been averagin' better than a man a day. They don't count the knifings."

"What?" exclaimed George Layton. "Oh come now, Arch. They said the same thing about Dodge City and I found it a pretty tame sort of place. A few shootings, but only below the deadline. Above the tracks, things were pretty quiet."

"There ain't no deadline here,"

declared Cummings. "We been waiting for you and Mr. Spence to get back, figurin' you'd put a stop to all this, but Spence says it's none of his business."

"He tell you we split, Arch?"

Cummings nodded. "Sorry to hear about it, too, Mr. Layton."

"You're working for *me*, Arch?"

"I always have, Mr. Layton."

"Good, I was counting on you. Uh, when did the Spences get back?"

"Day before yesterday. They've been sort of waiting for you, I guess."

"Yes? I thought our agreement was pretty clear. The line's to run right down the center of the valley, the east side for us, the west for them."

"I guess, he was meanin' Gunsight. It's on the east half . . . "

Layton frowned. "I don't understand?"

"The town's on your property."

"Is it? Well . . . " Layton shook his head quickly. "The question didn't come up when we were dividing. But a man can't own a town, can he? Or can he?"

"I wouldn't be knowin', Mr. Layton.

I'm ramroddin' your ranch."

"Yes! And how are we going to get out to this ranch?"

"Buckboard's right over there. They'll be holdin' supper . . ."

"Then let's get home!" cried Jill Layton.

The Layton house was five miles south of Gunsight, built on a gentle slope which had the best grass in all of Gunsight Valley. There was a spring near by which flowed down the slope and made a pond a half mile below.

The house itself was a rambling, sprawling one of red adobe bricks that had been plastered over with adobe mud. It had broad verandas and shade trees all around. To the right were several bunkhouses and beyond the bunkhouses, the corrals.

Mrs. Layton, a deep-bosomed woman of forty-five, was waiting on the veranda. She was a strong woman. At the close of the war between the states she had severed all her family ties and climbed into a wagon with her husband and small daughter and traveled fifteen hundred miles through wild country to settle in a land that boasted of less than one white person per hundred square miles. Jennie Layton had fought Indians in her time and was ready to fight them again.

Her reception of her daughter, whom she had not seen in a year, was an undemonstrative one, yet there was affection in her touch and glance and later, after dinner and a lengthy evening of conversation, she followed Jill to her room.

"What is it, Jill?" she asked.

"I – I don't know what you mean, Mother."

Mrs. Layton smiled. "You've been away a year, Jill. After all, I knew you for eighteen years. There's a look in your eye . . . who is he?"

"There isn't anyone. Oh, I met a few boys in St. Louis, naturally. But they seemed rather young when I compared them to the men around here."

"And there isn't one you've been thinking of, Jill?"

"No . . . but, Mother, I can't help

thinking about a man . . . the one who killed that bandit . . . ”

“Yes?”

“It – it was a shock . . . ”

“Of course; but this is Arizona, Jill. What about this man?”

“I met him before, under similar circumstances. I told father about the other time, but I didn’t tell him that this was the same man.”

“Why not, Jill?”

“Because . . . ” Jill Layton frowned. “I don’t know. Because I know his secret. He is . . . an outlaw.”

Mrs. Layton laughed shortly. “Arch went to Gunsight with me last Saturday while I did some shopping. Inside of five minutes he pointed out two known outlaws. And Andrew Spence stopped by only yesterday with a man named Temple, who gave me the shudders. If he isn’t a killer, I don’t . . . Anyway, Jill, you’re home now.” Mrs. Layton paused a moment, then added: “We won’t be going into Gunsight very often and with all the pickings they’ll have there, outlaws won't be coming around this ranch . . . You're tired, darling. Go to sleep."

In the living-room with the hardwood floor and the best furniture in Arizona east of Tucson, George Layton was waiting for his wife. As she came in and seated herself, he said:

"I don't like this, Jennie. I'm a cattleman and this is cattle country. Cattle and mining don't mix."

"That's what *you* think, George," Jennie Layton said, drily. "How many hands do you think you have on the payroll?"

"Arch told me coming out from Gunsight. The gold's got all but a dozen or so."

"Did Arch tell you that Andrew Spence has a full crew?"

"What?"

"He brought forty men back with him. They aren't all cowboys."

"I don't understand, Jennie."

"I don't either, George. What passed between you and Andy?"

George Layton sighed. "I never have

held anything back from you, Jennie. You know how Andy and I started this ranch. Our title to this land is negligible. Yes, we paid Don Carlos Gallegos a small sum of money for it. He claimed to hold it through an old Spanish grant. Actually, the land was his because no one else wanted it. Andy and I held it because no one dared take it away from us. We built up our herds . . . "

"Well, how did we build them up? Cattle that had been allowed to run wild during the war; mavericks that had worked their way west from the Pecos country; Mexican stuff that followed the water of the Rio Grande. We put our mark on it. The cattle didn't belong to anyone. It didn't matter as long as there was no market for it. But with steers bringing twenty dollars apiece up in Kansas we began shipping stock along the trail."

He paused and bit his lower lip. "Only we were shipping an inexhaustible supply, more head than I thought we could normally raise every year. All right, we don't know how many head we own, but certainly the increase couldn't be more than twenty thousand head a year . . . young stuff. The last three years we averaged thirty thousand head a year, sent up the trail . . . stock three to ten years old."

"Where did it come from, George?"

"That's why I broke up with Andy Spence. I asked him that same question and he couldn't answer it. But Manuel Higgins was in Dodge City with Andy."

"The Mexican bandit?"

"He isn't a Mexican. He was driven out of Texas by Captain McNelly of the Texas Rangers. The last five years he's been below the Border, with a gang of cut-throats that have terrorized all of Sonora. All the scum of Mexico and this country is with Higgins."

"So you suspect that Higgins has been running stolen Mexican cattle across the Rio Grande and having it sent with your herds – yours and Andy Spence's – to Kansas?"

"We sent eight herds up the trail

this last season; they totaled twenty-two thousand head. But Andy sold thirty-six thousand head in Dodge City. So I thought it best to dissolve partnership. I took the east half of the valley and twelve thousand head. Andy was quite reasonable about it . . ."

"That was before he knew about Gunsight."

"How will that affect things?"

"Gold and silver. One of the mines is down a hundred feet and hit silver, worth twelve thousand dollars to the ton. The mines are in the east half of the valley."

"But, Jennie," protested George Layton, "mineral rights belong to whoever finds them. Even if I had an indisputable title to this ranch, I couldn't prevent anyone from claiming the mineral rights . . . "

"There are no less than twenty lawyers in Gunsight," said Jennie Layton. "Even if the town is less than sixty days old. I talked to one last week. He said the owner of the land has a claim to a percentage of all minerals taken therefrom. He's willing to start suit."

"What? They've got a court here?"

"They held elections last week. Gunsight has a mayor; two judges and a sheriff appointed by the territorial governor. This part of the valley has been cut off from Piñon County and is a county by itself. Oro Grande County."

George Layton stared at his wife in consternation for several minutes.

6

LIQUOR did things to nerves. Harvey Dawson never drank and had always disapproved of his men imbibing. But the day had been hot – and strenuous. The saloon was a sanctuary to Jim Parker and the natural thing to do in a saloon was to drink.

So he ordered a glass of beer, at the pine plank bar of the O.K. Saloon & Dance Hall. He drank the cool, refreshing beer, then turned and suryeyed the big room. It was about forty by sixty feet in size. A bar ran down the entire length of the room. The rear half of the room was supposed to be a dance floor. There was a violinist, an accordionist and a man who clanked cymbals together, for an orchestra. Percentage girls danced with ragged, bearded miners and sunburned cowboys.

The front part of the saloon was

entirely devoted to gambling. There were chuck-a-luck cages, faro layouts, poker tables, dice and even a roulette wheel.

There were more than a hundred patrons in the room. Yet, in this crowd, Mike Megan, the stage driver, found Jim Parker. With him was a somber-faced man in a Prince Albert.

"Smith," cried the stage driver, "shake hands with my brother, Josh. He's eddicated. He came here ten days ago to hang out his shingle as a lawyer and last week he was made a judge. My brother, Judge Megan."

Judge Megan held out his hand gravely to Parker. "This is a strange country. How do you do. Mike told me about the bandit you killed. His name was Terry Walker. His brother, Ben, is a resident of our thriving city and was undoubtedly the man with Terry. I want you to identify him when he shows up here, as he probably will."

"I'm sorry, Judge Megan," Parker said. "He wore a mask."

"But you shot him, Mike says. If

Ben shows up here wounded, he's your man."

"An identification like that wouldn't stand up, would it?"

"It would in my court, Smith," said Judge Megan testily. "This is a boom town, but it's the foulest place in this entire United States. Murderers and thieves intimidate honest people here. I was appointed a judge by the governor and I intend to live up to my oath, regardless of what other judicial appointees do."

Parker looked thoughtfully at Judge Megan. Then he smiled faintly at the judge's stage-driver brother. "I'm a stranger here, I came hoping to find a gold mine."

Megan regarded Parker coldly. "From what Mike said about you I'd hoped . . . well, it doesn't matter." The judge turned away abruptly.

His place was taken instantly by a man wearing a floppy black hat and an incredibly dirty linen duster that came to his ankles. The pockets on each side sagged heavily.

"So you're the lad that dusted the big, bad bandit? By tomorrow you'd better be scarce because if it was Terry Walker, Ben'll nail your hide to the wall."

Parker turned away deliberately and signaled to the bartender. "Another beer, please."

"Beer!" jeered the man in the linen duster.

Jim Parker struck him in the throat with the edge of his palm. He followed through on the swing and as the man was choking smashed him in the face with his fist.

The man in the duster reeled back and would have fallen but for the helping hand of a swarthy, sardonic man who wore two Frontier Models.

"Easy, Johnny," the sardonic man said.

Johnny sputtered in his rage. He struck off the hands that were holding him and snarled at Jim Parker, "Reach for your hardware!" His hands touched the pockets of his linen coat.

Parker said, "If your hands go into those pockets, I'll kill you."

"That's what I'm aiming to do to you. I'm giving you a square deal. I've got two guns in my pockets and my name is Johnny Shade. Reach!"

"Reach yourself, Johnny Shade," Parker said, softly.

"Hold it, Johnny!" snapped the sardonic man. "You can fight later. I want to talk to this man."

"Talk quick, Fletch," Johnny Shade said, "because I'm going to kill him when he moves."

The man called Fletch suddenly wrapped his arms about Johnny Shade, pinning his hands to his sides. He grinned wolfishly at Parker over Shade's shoulder.

"Run now if you want, mister."

Shade was fighting Fletch, but the swarthy man was much too strong for him. Jim Parker watched the tableau for a moment, then reached for his glass of beer. He drank half of it slowly, then put the glass back on the bar.

He saw Johnny Shade go limp in Fletch's grip, and the latter released him. Shade stabbed his right index finger, at Parker. "You're a pilgrim; you don't know who I am."

"You said your name was Johnny Shade. Mine's Smith."

"Smith," said the man who had been holding Shade. "I'm Fletch Hobbs. Let's have a talk."

"You're talking now."

"No," said Hobbs, jerking his head. "Over there."

He started into the crowd and a path was somehow opened for him. Shade remained at the bar, his smoldering eyes on Parker. The latter shrugged and followed Hobbs.

In the corner a table had been strangely vacated. Hobbs took a stool with his back to the wall and smiled at Parker. The smile did not reach his eyes.

Parker hesitated, then sat down with his back facing the room. He almost never sat that way in public.

"You really never heard of Johnny

Shade?" Hobbs began.

"No. And I never saw a man carry guns in the pockets of a linen coat."

"No one does except Johnny. He would have killed you."

"Perhaps."

"Not perhaps – certainly. I saved your life because I liked your nerve."

"It didn't take nerve – if I didn't know Johnny Shade."

"I wonder," said Fletch Hobbs. "Perhaps you'd have stood up to him just the same, even if you knew he was the deadliest man in Arizona, but one."

"Who is deadlier . . . you?"

"Bull's-eye," said Fletch Hobbs, smiling again his humorless smile. "I'm the only man can handle Johnny and sometimes I get doubtful when he's in one of his crazy moods. He was reading all afternoon."

Parker raised eyebrows and Hobbs nodded.

"Look at him. He hasn't washed in three days, shaved in a week and a goat wouldn't wear that dirty coat, yet Johnny's a graduate of that Harvard

College they've got in the East." Hobbs laughed. "I could take a petition through this room right now and get it full of crosses. The mayor of Gunsight has to make his mark. And Johnny Shade is a college man . . . What's your name, Smith?"

"Smith. Jim Smith."

"All right, you're going to stick to that name. Then why'd you kill Terry Walker?"

"He wanted my money."

"Did you have any?"

"Two hundred dollars."

Hobbs stared at Parker. "For two hundred dollars you pulled a sleeve-gun on Terry and Ben Walker? And your name is Smith?"

"Look, Hobbs," said Parker, "how does all this concern you?"

Hobbs grimaced. "That's right, you're a stranger around here. Ever hear of Manuel Higgins?"

"No."

"Then you *have* come a long way. But you met George Layton on the stage. Layton and his partner, Andy Spence, were the biggest men in this country – until this strike. Me and Johnny Shade worked for them." He grinned. "We're cowboys. But we're not working for them, now."

"You're miners?" Parker asked in a tone of polite boredom.

"Well, we're after gold, so I guess you might call us miners."

"I see," said Parker. "I think I'll have another glass of beer."

"Wait a minute," snapped Hobbs. "I'm not through. You call yourself Smith and you're handy with a gun – a sleeve-gun, at least. But you're not a gambler, because you'd be in a game by now. So what the hell are you?"

Parker did not answer. Johnny Shade had finally come through the crowd and stood a few feet away, glowering down at Parker.

Parker asked, deliberately: "What's your proposition, Hobbs?"

"Tomorrow you'll find out there aren't any claims around Gunsight. But that shouldn't worry you. There's plenty of jobs open at four dollars a day."

"So you're offering me a better paying job?"

"No," said Johnny Shade.

"Yes," said Fletch Hobbs.

Parker was spared answering, for at that moment a commotion broke out at the bar. Men began yelling and scrambling back. A gun roared and a man's voice rose: "Yip-yip-yipee!" The gun banged again and again, until it was emptied. Adobe plaster from the ceiling showered down upon the bar.

"Kearney Spence," said Fletch Hobbs. "Feeling his oats."

"Watch it," said Johnny Shade. "Plennert is going to do something. Twenty dollars he backs down, Fletch."

"Bet!"

Hobbs and Shade hurried across the room. There was plenty of space, for almost everyone in the vicinity of the bar had backed away. A number of cautious patrons had even crawled under tables.

A tall, lean man with long mustaches had stopped inside the door and was looking at Kearney Spence, who, Parker noted, was a wild-looking youth of about twenty-one, although rather well built.

There was a nickeled badge on the vest of Plennert. He said, "Kearney, you hadn't ought to do that. I told you yesterday . . ."

"Stop me," taunted Spence. He suddenly sheathed his emptied revolver in his left holster and held his hand poised over the right. Plennert saw the stance and a frown came to his face.

"Don't you try anythin', Kearney," he said. "I'm the marshal of Gunsight and it's my duty to preserve law and order."

"Marshal," said Kearney Spence, "go crawl in your hole, before I chase you there, like I did a marshal up in Kansas."

Plennert tugged at his mustache. It was apparent that he didn't know what to do. Johnny Shade's voice cut the sudden stillness: "You lose, Fletch, he backed down."

Jim Parker got up from the table and started toward Hobbs and Shade. Before he reached them Fletch Hobbs snarled at Plennert.

"You yellow coward, I bet twenty dollars you wouldn't back down. Go and take him, or I'll bust your head open myself."

Young Kearney Spence shot a quick look at Hobbs. "Hey, Fletch, you're sidin' against me!"

"I got a bet on . . . Are you going to take him, Plennert?"

The marshal seemed to shrink. It was evident that he was even more afraid of Fletch Hobbs than he was of Kearney Spence. He shuffled forward.

"Put up your — "

"Stop!" cried Kearney. "One step more and I'll drill you!"

Fletch Hobbs stepped around behind the marshal and gave him a sudden, violent shove. Plennert screamed as he toppled forward. Instinctively, he clawed for his gun.

Kearney Spence's hand snaked to his

gun. He got it clear of the holster while the marshal was still groping for his own. The gun thundered and Plennert spun around and pitched to the floor.

Then realization seemed to sober Kearney Spence and he stared down stupidly at the man he had just shot. "What . . . what . . . " he mumbled.

"I win," Fletch Hobbs said softly to Johnny Shade.

"He's dead," Jim Parker said, just behind Hobbs. "You murdered him."

"What's that?" cried Hobbs, whirling.

"I said you murdered him."

"All right, for the sake of argument, say I murdered him. What are you going to do about it?"

"Nothing, Plennert's dead."

"Wait a minute."

Judge Megan, the brother of the stagecoach driver, came out of the crowd. He was shoving along a bleary-eyed, fat man of about fifty.

"Mayor Wiley saw the whole thing," the judge said. "It was cold-blooded murder. Wiley, arrest the three of them."

"Wh-what?" stammered the bleary-eyed mayor of Gunsight. "I c-can't arrest anyone."

"The devil you can't. You're the mayor. And if you'll bring them into my court I'll see that they receive their just deserts."

Fletch Hobbs turned and looked thoughtfully at Judge Megan. Then he spat deliberately at his feet. "It was self-defense," he said. "Plennert pulled a gun on the kid."

"Yes," exclaimed Mayor Wiley. "That's what it was — self-defense."

"You drunken oaf!" cried Judge Megan. "If you don't arrest these men I'll go to the governor tomorrow and see that you're removed from office and go to jail along with these men."

"But it's up to the marshal to arrest people. The marshal's dead."

"Then appoint another — and see that he arrests these men." The judge's eyes swung around to settle on Jim Parker. His lip curled, then his eyes narrowed.

"Smith! Will you take the job?"

Parker was taken aback. "Me . . . a marshal?"

"The job pays two hundred a month . . . and three dollars for every arrest."

"Yeah," said Fletch Hobbs. "You can get three dollars for arresting me. And three for Johnny Shade."

Johnny Shade's eyes were glowing. "Take the job, Smith, because I figure to kill you anyway."

Parker made a downward brushing movement, and his long-barreled Frontier Model appeared in his hand. "I'll take the job," he said. "Now reach into those pockets, Johnny Shade!"

Hobbs and Shade were both caught flat-footed. But Johnny Shade leaned forward and his hands crept slowly to his pockets. Fletch Hobbs seemed to lean away from Shade, and his feet slipped to the left a few inches.

"Another inch and you're a dead man," said Parker. "And you, Johnny."

The barrel of Parker's Colt flicked upward suddenly and connected with

Johnny Shade's jaw. As the killer fell forward Parker took a step forward and sidewards, caught Shade with his left hand and, using his body as a shield, poked his revolver over Shade's shoulder.

Fletch Hobbs' gun had just cleared leather, but the gunman froze when he saw the small target that Parker was making. He swore softly and let the gun clatter to the floor.

"All right, Smith, this time . . ."

Parker let the unconscious Shade slip to the floor. He stepped back and included Kearney Spence in the sweep of his revolver. "All right, you two, pick him up and carry him to the jail. Judge Megan, will you show the way?"

A hum went suddenly through the crowded saloon as the tension was broken. Its pitch heightened until it became a roar.

The jail was a block from the saloon. It was the top floor of a two-story adobe building. The first floor contained the Gunsight General Store.

The room was about twenty by thirty feet in size. The rear half was divided from the front by a wall of crisscrossed strap-iron which had a door in the center. The only furnishings in the rear were a few filthy blankets. In front, there were a rough table and a couple of chairs. Evidently this was supposed to be the "office" for the town marshal and jailer. Only there was no jailer. There were keys on the table, however, and Judge Megan and Parker locked the prisoners into their section. As the door was closed on them, Fletch Hobbs said, "Have your fun now. Our turn comes in the morning and don't you forget it!"

"You'll have your turn," Judge Megan said, grimly. He turned to Parker. "Are you going to stay here tonight?"

"Is it the job of the marshal to guard the prisoners?"

"No, but we haven't had many so far. In the morning I'll see that the mayor employs a jailer. I just want to say that I appreciate your taking this job. After my brother told me what you had done on the stage I knew you were the man this town needed and you can count on my support to the last ditch. You can . . . ”

He stopped as a fist pounded on the door which led to the outside flight of stairs running down to the street. The door was kicked inwards and an angry-faced, gray-bearded man pushed abruptly in.

“Kearney!” he cried.

Kearney Spence winced. “Hello, Pop.”

Andrew Spence glowered at Judge Megan. “I just heard about this. I'm Andrew Spence.”

“Glad to meet you,” Judge Megan said, icily. “To that I'd like to add that I don't think you're much of a father, letting a young squirt like — ”

Andy Spence let out a bellow. “Why, you sanctimonious law-spoutin' hypocrite, turn loose my son, or by Geronimo, I'll tear down this two-bit jail and break it over your skull.”

“Mr. Spence,” said Judge Megan, “I'd

advise you to leave at once and engage an attorney to defend your son in the morning. The charge is murder and if he is found guilty he will be hanged. I give you my solemn promise as to that!"

Spence opened his mouth to blast the judge once more, but only air came from it. Then he whirled and stamped out of the room. Jim Parker heard his boots pound on the stairs.

"Good night," said Judge Megan. "I'll see you in the morning, Marshal Smith!"

He went to the door, stepped out — and a shotgun blasted the night. Shot rattled against the door-jamb and bounced into the room.

Aghast, Jim Parker leaped to the door. His foot caught on the body of Judge Megan. The light from inside the jail showed him the thing that had been the judge's face.

A horse's hoofs rang out on the street below. They were going past the general store, out of range of Parker's gun.

Pursuit was futile. Parker had no horse. By the time he could commandeer one, the assassin would either be lost in the town or have cleared it.

From behind the bars Fletcher Hobbs' voice called: "How do you like your new job, Marshal?"

7

A half-hour after Judge Megan had been killed a delegation came to Gunsight jail. It consisted of three men: bleary-eyed sodden Mayor Wiley, a walrus-mustached man wearing a somewhat rusty silk hat who was introduced as Judge Anderson, and a little, weasel-faced man who the others said was Harold Grigsby, sheriff of Oro Grande County.

"Too bad about Judge Megan," Judge Anderson said, shaking his head. "I suppose you'll get the man who killed him, Sheriff Grigsby?"

"Of course," said the sheriff. "Come morning and I'll be working on it."

"Good!" nodded the judge. "And now I may as well try the prisoners. Marshal Smith, will you state the charges?"

For a moment, Jim Parker, alias Smith, regarded Judge Anderson through slitted eyes. Then he shrugged. "Murder."

"Murder? Well! That's a serious charge. Kearney Spence, you've heard the charge. What have you got to say?"

"He pulled a gun on me first," young Spence said, sullenly.

"Is that true, Marshal Smith?"

"As far as it goes. Spence was creating a disturbance. The marshal asked him to stop and Spence challenged him. Hobbs and Shade made a bet, the latter betting that Plennert would back down. Plennert did back down — "

"Wait a minute," cut in Judge Anderson. "All that's beside the point. Which of them drew first — Plennert or Spence?"

"Plennert, but — "

"That right, Mayor Wiley? You were a witness."

"S'right," muttered the mayor.

"A clear-cut case of self-defense," declared Judge Anderson. "The prisoner is acquitted, but he is fined twenty-five dollars for discharging a gun in public. Next case, Fletcher Hobbs!"

"The charge is murder," said Parker, "but let it slide."

"Eh?"

"Why waste time? You know damn well you're going to acquit them."

"That's contempt of court, Smith!" snapped Judge Anderson. "Another such remark and I'll fine you."

Jim Parker gave the judge a contemptuous glance and walked out of the building. Down on the street he walked a half-block until he came to a building which had a sign: "Hotel." The hotel consisted of one large room in which were a number of wooden bunks.

He rented one of the beds for two dollars, paying in advance. He went to bed with all his clothes on, like the other hotel "guests."

In the morning he washed at the communal washbasin and went out to see Gunsight.

It looked worse than it had the evening before. The street was rutted and cut up by countless wagons and horses. Refuse was seemingly thrown out into the streets by the residents. At the west end a slag dump protruded twenty feet into the street.

It was only seven o'clock, but early as it was, the street teemed with activity. Across the street from the O.K. Saloon & Dance Hall, Parker saw a sign over a new frame building: *Eats.*

He went in and sat down at one of three long, rough tables. There were only two customers in the place at the time. One of them was Mayor Wiley. Parker chose one of the other tables.

A waitress came through a swinging door. She wore a skirt of heavy material, a man's woolen shirt and cowboy boots. She was in her early twenties and had soft dark hair. She was not exactly pretty, but her features were even and her complexion clear. Then she smiled at Parker and a transition seemed to come over her face until it was actually beautiful.

"Good morning, customer!" she said cheerily. "I can give you flapjacks and ham or ham and flapjacks. And coffee."

"How about ham and eggs?"

"If you furnish the eggs. Or if you bring the hen, I'll give you eggs as long as she lays. Mmm, maybe our Number Two breakfast will suit you better. It costs fifty cents more."

"What is it?"

"Ham and flapjacks, but with it I sing *Buffalo Gals.*"

Jim Parker chuckled in spite of himself. "The Number One breakfast will do."

The girl winked. "A wise choice. I'm a very bad singer."

She went to the kitchen.

Behind Parker a chair scraped the floor and Mayor Wiley came over. "Look, Smith, I couldn't help what happened last night. I didn't want to be mayor or anythin', but the boys insisted and now they won't let me quit."

"I think you make a very good mayor," said Parker. "For Gunsight, where they figure a man's life is worth twenty-five dollars."

Wiley looked as if he were about to burst into tears. "'Tain't my fault. This is a hard country, the Apaches on the warpath, outlaws from across the Rio Grande and gunfighters right here in Gunsight. I wouldn't want to be marshal of this town, nohow."

"Nor do I."

"You mean that? You're resignin'?"

"I resigned last night."

Mayor Wiley sighed in relief. "You're much better off. If you could keep outa the way of Fletch Hobbs and Johnny Shade, I think they'd forget it in a few days."

"I've a very short memory myself. I've already forgotten that I met those gentlemen."

"Fine! Uh, I'll talk to them. Uh, good mornin'."

He put a silver dollar on the table and hurried out of the restaurant. The other customer had already gone and Parker was alone when the waitress brought him his food.

"Did I hear our mayor talking to you?" she asked, as she put the plates before Parker.

"Hizzoner," laughed Parker.

"I heard. D'you mind? I didn't know you were the man who – who did what you did. It was pretty swell, but you haven't got a chance. Take a tip from an old-timer in Gunsight. Get on your horse and leave, right after you eat."

"I haven't got a horse."

"Then walk. You'll be safer on foot, surrounded by Apaches, than you will be here in Gunsight. I know."

Parker cut off a piece of ham, chewed on it, then looked up. "What's your name?"

"Ethel Halsted. And your name is Smith, I hear. John?"

"Jim. How long have you worked here?"

"I opened one week after gold was discovered here. I had a place in Tucson that wasn't doing very well. The climate in Missouri didn't agree with me."

"Missouri! Why – "

"*You're* from Missouri?" Ethel Halsted exclaimed.

Parker hesitated and then nodded.

"Boonville." Which was a lie, but he had been in Boonville and could cover up sufficiently well if she carried it too far.

"Boonville! Why, we're practically neighbors. I'm from Higginsville." She grimaced. "That's in the outlaw country. They say Dawson hangs around there sometimes."

"Harvey Dawson?" Parker asked cautiously. "Did you ever see him in Missouri?"

"I don't know. No one's ever seen Harvey Dawson who'll admit it. They've never had a picture or even a description of him. Only one of his men has ever been captured and he escaped. I was reading about it in the papers just last week." Her eyes were on Jim Parker, but showed no alarm or unusual excitement. "His name is supposed to be Jim Parker."

Parker finished his food and put a dollar on the table. He pushed back his chair. "That was a fine breakfast."

"Thanks, Missouri. But look, even, even though I hate to lose a customer, take that advice I gave you. Fletcher Hobbs and Johnny Shade are bad medicine."

Parker grinned. "I'll think about it."

He left the restaurant and stood outside for a minute looking up the street. Gunsight was beginning to show a little more activity.

George Layton came out of an adobe hut across the street. A tall, well-built man of about thirty, clean-shaven in this land where hirsutial adornment was the vogue, followed and shook hands. Then he nodded across the street in Parker's direction and Layton jerked around.

Parker turned to walk up the street, but Layton called to him. "Oh, Smith! Marshal Smith!"

Parker walked across the street. "Smith, we were just talking about you. Shake hands with Mr. Richard Pendleton, who is the editor and publisher of *The Gunsight Target.*"

"Dick Pendleton is the name," grinned the young newspaper editor. "You'll be interested in the lead article in this week's issue. It's just been set up in type and if you'll step inside I'll be glad to show you a proof. It concerns last night's events."

Parker shook his head. "No."

"What do you mean – no?" cried George Layton. "You're the man of the hour in this town."

Parker squinted at Dick Pendleton. "Are you up to the minute on events?"

"Certainly. I know about the shindy they ran on you last night. That's what the article is about – a blast at the crooked element in Gunsight and a rousing appeal for the citizens to get behind the town marshal."

"That's it. I'm not marshal any more."

"What!" cried both Pendleton and Layton.

"I've been asked to resign. By the mayor. Naturally, I did."

"But you can't!" cried Pendleton. "You were the first man to come to this town who had the courage to stand up to Fletcher Hobbs and Johnny Shade. And after what you did on the stagecoach yesterday, why – why you're the one man Gunsight needs. Judge Megan had the vision and the force, but he was powerless without someone to do the physical combat."

Parker shrugged. "I was on the spot last night, in a position where I couldn't back down. But I wouldn't make a marshal, even if your local administration wanted me which it doesn't."

Layton groaned. "I only returned to Gunsight yesterday, after an absence of almost three months, but what I've seen — and heard — in this short while has disconcerted me greatly. The situation is intolerable and I intend to do something about it . . . Do you know that the entire town of Gunsight is on my property?"

"No," said Parker, in surprise. "I hadn't known."

"Well, it is. Andy Spence and myself owned this entire valley. When we dissolved the partnership he took the western half and I the eastern. The line runs two miles west of Gunsight, so I own all this land."

"Including the mines?"

Layton shrugged. "That's a legal question. Perhaps the mineral rights belong to whoever finds and works the minerals. But certainly, the townsite is on my property. So I believe I have some rights and say in how this town is run."

"I'm backing you, Mr. Layton," said Dick Pendleton.

"Good. This town will need an honest newspaper. But it needs honest town officials, too. And from what I've heard there isn't a single one. Is there, Pendleton?"

"I haven't seen any of them walking around with lanterns."

"What about the sheriff?"

Pendleton screwed up his face. "Hal Grigsby? A good man . . . if he wore a handkerchief over his face."

"Then we *have* got our work cut out for us. That's why we need you so much, Smith."

Parker frowned. I don't see how I can be of any use. The sheriff, the mayor and the one remaining judge are all opposed to me."

"Wait!" cried Layton. "The judges are appointed by the territorial governor. Judge Megan has to be replaced. If we can get another honest judge . . . "

"Exactly!" exclaimed Pendleton. "I'll send a copy of *The Target* to the governor. It'll show him how conditions in Gunsight really are."

"I'Il *take* the paper to him," declared Layton. "I'll stay with him until he makes the appointment. We're going to get to work here."

8

JILL LAYTON had forgotten how peaceful it was in Gunsight Valley. She had gone to St. Louis for a year because her mother had wanted it. But Jill hadn't really liked it. She'd gone to a fine school and had attended a number of receptions and balls, and all the time she had been there she had felt ill at ease.

This was what she loved and wanted. She rose before seven and put on a tan riding skirt and blouse. She found a pair of soft elkskin boots that still fitted her and after breakfast went to explore the ranchyard.

She found it strangely quiet. In the old days there had been a hustle and bustle. Even though half of the hands were sheltered at the Spence place five miles away, the force had been so large that there were seldom less than a hundred men in the vicinity of the

Layton bunkhouses.

Of course, most of them were out on the range now, but even so there should have been a dozen or so around. She found Ming in the help's kitchen and after a while located Dugan the blacksmith by the sound of a hammer on a horseshoe.

But the bunkhouses were deserted. Even Arch Cummings, the foreman, was gone. There were only a few horses in the corrals.

Somewhat disappointed, Jill returned to the cool, broad veranda of the ranchhouse and was about to seat herself when she heard the *clop–clop* of horses' hoofs and saw two riders approaching. The foremost was galloping his horse a hundred yards ahead of the other who was riding at a trot.

"Yip-ee!" cried the first rider, bringing his horse up in a cloud of dust.

It was Kearney Spence. Jill had not heard of his adventure of the evening before, but she recalled Dodge City and her greeting was not as warm as it would have been otherwise.

"How are you, Kearney?" she said quietly.

"How am I? Hey, that's a fine way to greet your sweetheart after being away for a year."

Kearney bounced down from his horse and would have embraced Jill, except that she stepped back. He scowled.

"I hear you were in Dodge for a day and didn't even let me know."

"Why," said Jill, "I understand you were in the calaboose all the time I was there."

Kearney flushed. "Your father told you. I suppose he told you about last night, too."

"No, he didn't. What . . . ?"

"Well, you'll hear it soon enough, so I may as well tell you. The Yankee Marshal pulled a gun on me and naturally I had to protect myself."

"Kearney!" gasped Jill. "You did not . . . "

"What could I do? It was self-defense. Judge Anderson and Mayor Wiley both saw it. Say, what's so awful about that? Times have changed around here. Gunsight's a pretty salty place. You ought to see it."

"I did, last night, when I came in. I — I don't like it."

Kearney Spence chuckled. "Too strong, eh? Me, I think it's exciting. Better'n Dodge. No need to go there now. We can sell most of the cattle we want right here . . . Dave . . ." the last to the second rider who had come up, but remained on his horse. "Jill, this is Dave Temple, our new foreman."

"Howdy, miss," said Dave Temple, raising his hat and grinning sardonically.

Jill looked at him and a tiny shiver ran through her. Dave Temple had the coldest, palest blue eyes of any person she had ever seen. He wasn't much older probably than Kearney Spence, but his expression was worldly-wise. Jill suspected he had lived much.

She nodded and murmured an acknowledgment of the introduction. "Dave's sorta acting as my bodyguard," Kearney

Spence explained. "Funny, isn't it? But Dad insisted. Said he didn't like the looks of that new marshal they've got in Gunsight. A killer, I understand. The one who was on the stage with you and shot the holdup man when he wasn't looking."

Jill exclaimed, "Jim Smith? Did you say he was the new *marshal* of Gunsight?"

"As of last night. But Dad says he's going to have him fired today. He would've killed me last night if I hadn't guessed what he was up to. But Dave'll handle him. Eh, Dave?"

"Yeah, sure," replied Dave Temple nonchalantly.

"You mean there was . . . the new marshal was involved in your escapade last night?" Jill persisted. "He was the man you shot?"

"No – no, that was Plennert. It was a mixup all around. Johnny Shade and Flesh Hobbs were egging this Plennert on to drawing on me. Naturally I had to protect myself. So then Judge Megan had to butt in, and first thing you know he'd forced Mayor Wiley into appointing this Smith marshal to take Plennert's place. Well, I knew that Smith was a killer, so I went along to the jail. This Megan kept yelling and shouting all evening, so somebody took a crack at him — "

"*You,* Kearney?" Jill cried.

"Naw, I was still inside jail when it happened. Nobody knows who did it. But the guy'd been shouting off in Gunsight ever since he got here and plenty of people had it in for him. So then Judge Anderson took over and naturally, since he and Mayor Wiley had witnessed the whole thing, turned me loose. This killer Smith got pretty sore and so . . ." he nodded to Dave Temple, "so Dad told Dave to ride around with me a while."

Jill Layton shook her head in bewilderment. "This is all too much for me, Kearney. Will you — excuse me? I've got a headache."

"Hey!" cried Kearney Spence, annoyed. "I rode all the way over just to talk to you. I mean, there's a big dance in

Gunsight tonight and naturally I want to take you."

"But I just reached home last night."

"You've had a night's sleep. I'll be around for you. All right?"

To get rid of him, Jill agreed. Then she hurried into the house. Jennie Layton looked up from some mending she was doing. "That was Kearney Spence, wasn't it?"

Jill threw herself into a big, easy chair. "He's changed, Mother. Horribly! Even in Dodge City . . . but I thought that was just exuberance. They say all the cowboys cut loose in Dodge. But I didn't think . . ."

"Gunsight is Dodge City brought home," Mrs. Layton said quietly.

Jill stared at her mother. "That's what Kearney said!"

"Well, it's true, Jill. I'm wondering if it wouldn't have been better for you to have remained in St. Louis."

"No!" Jill exclaimed. "This is home. It's the only place I want to be. I guess – I guess we'll just have to do our best to make it the sort of home we want."

Mrs. Layton smiled fondly at her daughter. "Then you'll go to the ball tonight?"

"Yes."

A speculative gleam came into Mrs. Layton's eyes. She had met Dick Pendleton, the young newspaperman, a week ago. She wondered how her daughter would react when she met him. Pendleton would be at the dance, no doubt.

Then George Layton came home at noon and announced that he was going to the territorial capital on the early evening stage. Both Jill and her mother were dismayed.

"But we'd counted on your taking us to the dance this evening," Mrs. Layton said.

"What dance?"

"The Gold Dance. It's to be a sort of get-together, to celebrate the success of the gold mines. Everyone will be at the dance. Many of the mining engineers have brought their families. The business men of the town and — well, everyone!"

"I'm sorry," said George Layton. "Some very important matters have come up and I can't delay a day. I must see the governor. But there's no reason for you not to go to the dance. Arch Cummings can drive you and I suppose it'll be all right while you're there. Uh, there's an attorney in Gunsight I've retained to handle some matters for me. His name is Kennard and he strikes me as a rather substantial person; I'll have him introduce himself at the dance!"

Layton frowned as he regarded his daughter. "And I suppose young Pendleton will attend. He's a chap puts out the newspaper. Likely chap and seems to come from a good family. He's helping me in this business. Keep young Spence away, Jill. He's gone down pretty fast."

"I'm afraid I can't keep him away tonight, Dad," Jill said. "You see, he was here this morning and I agreed to go to the dance with him."

George Layton exclaimed angrily,

"After what he did last night he had the nerve to come here this morning? I'll tell him something. I'm glad I broke with his father. Kearney'll come to no good end. In fact, if my mission to the capital is successful, he may yet find himself in a great deal of trouble."

"Did he actually kill a man last night?"

"He boasted about it? Then he *has* gone down a long way. Yes, he killed a man; in cold blood, too, I understand from reliable witnesses. If it hadn't been for that fellow from the stage, the one who killed the bandit, no telling what would have happened."

Jill shuddered a little. "This Smith, wh-who is he, Father?"

Layton shrugged. "No one knows. He won't talk about himself. But he's the fire Gunsight needs. A man who isn't afraid of anything."

Jill bit her lip. "From the little I've seen of him – I mean, what do you think of him?"

"Just what I said. I wouldn't be a bit

surprised if he's a man on the dodge. Certainly he's as handy with guns as any of these so-called bad men. But if we can get him on our side, he'll be invaluable."

"You mean, as a hired killer?"

"Eh? What put that notion into your head, Jill?"

"You say he's probably an outlaw; you know he killed that bandit yesterday; yet you want to use him as marshal of Gunsight."

"You've got to fight fire with fire. I understand he bluffed both Johnny Shade and Fletch Hobbs – and young Spence to boot. Of course he didn't know how deadly Shade and Hobbs actually were, but somehow I believe he wouldn't have cared. I think he's the most dangerous man I've ever known anywhere."

It was on the tip of Jill's tongue to reveal Jim Parker's identity, but she stopped. Why, she didn't know.

9

IN Gunsight, Jim Parker spent the day getting acquainted. A conspicuous figure the moment he had stepped off the stagecoach the evening before, he had been made famous by his brief regime as town marshal.

After talking with George Layton and Dick Pendleton, he discovered that be had absolutely nothing to do in Gunsight. He couldn't hang around his hotel; it was a mere bunkhouse. He went to the O.K. Saloon & Dance Hall, had a glass of beer and discovered a three-handed poker game going on.

He went over to watch and learned quickly that the soft-handed man in a Prince Albert was much too clever with his hands for the other players, both of whom were roughly dressed men with calloused hands. Yet the stakes were high.

After he had watched a few minutes the professional gambler snapped irritably at Parker. "If you want to sit in sit down; if not, go somewhere else."

"I'll sit in a few hands, if you don't mind."

The gambler grunted. "Table stakes. My name's Morland."

"Mine's Smith."

The gambler's eyes popped wide open. "Smith! Not – "

Parker shrugged and brought out his money. He put ten dollars back into his pocket and stacked up the remainder, a hundred and eighty dollars.

It was Morland's deal. Parker got a pair of sixes, but when one of the players opened for a dollar and was raised five by Morland, Parker threw in his cards. He detected a slight sneer on the gambler's lips.

Morland won the pot finally, some thirty dollars.

The player on Parker's right dealt the next hand. Parker got a pair of queens, an ace, a seven and a trey. He frowned at the hand, picked up a dollar, then added another.

"I open for two dollars."

The man on Parker's left called. Morland raised it five. The dealer dropped out. Parker hesitated over the five-dollar raise and finally threw in his cards.

The other player also quit and Morland raked in the small pot. In doing so he managed to raise up and tip over Parker's hand. The curl of his lip became more pronounced as he saw the queens.

It was Parker's deal now. He gave himself a complete bust, but the man on his left opened for a dollar and was raised the usual five by Morland. The third player called Morland's raise and retaliated with a twenty-dollar tilt of his own.

That made it twenty-six dollars up to Parker. He counted out the money. "Ah," said Morland. "Mr. Smith has a hand."

The man who had opened contented himself with calling and Morland said: "Two cards, please!"

The first man drew only one, indicating, since he had opened, two pairs. Either that or he was breaking his openers and trying for a flush or straight. After looking at his one card, he held his hand.

Parker gave two cards to Morland and three to the man who had raised Morland twenty dollars. Then he put down the pack. "I'll play these," he announced quietly.

Three pairs of eyes came quickly to his face and the man on his left contented himself with betting a dollar. Morland scowled at his hand, looked at Parker, then raised the bet five dollars. The man on Parker's right tossed in his hand. "Beats my kings."

Parker counted all his money. "One hundred and thirty-seven dollars. Table stakes you said, Mr. Morland."

The player on his left swore and tossed in his cards. "My two pair are no good in this."

Morland fanned his cards, riffled them and fanned them open again. "The way you've been playing them, Smith, you've got a full house or an ace-high flush. Which beats three queens." He threw in his hand.

Parker tossed in his cards and began gathering in the money. Morland reached out and turned over Parker's hand. Noting that the hand didn't even contain a pair, he cried out in consternation, "What the devil kind of playing you call that?"

"You didn't pay to see, that hand, Morland," Parker said coolly. "Deal me out."

"What?" cried Morland. "You'd quit when you're ahead?"

"That's the time to quit. Any objections?"

"No," said Morland. "None . . . " His hand made a quick movement toward his vest. At the instant Parker's hands were both on the table, straightening his winnings. His right hand flicked forward, slapped Morland in the face. Morland started to fall backwards with his chair, his hand still clawing for his vest pocket.

Parker carried a vest gun himself and knew its lethal qualities. He had used it the day before on the stage bandit, Terry Walker. He followed through with his blow, jerking up the table with his knees and then spilling it over on top of Morland.

Morland cried out in pain, but finally reached his derringer. The little gun came out . . . and then Parker's Frontier Model roared and a bullet crashed into the floor an inch from Morland's right elbow.

"Drop it, Morland!" he cried.

With the muzzle of the little gun almost pointing at Parker, the gambler's eyes met Parker's. They held for a fraction of a second, then the derringer clattered to the floor. Parker walked around and kicked it clear across the room.

"Nice work," said a voice at the bar. "They said you was a rootin'-tootin' sonofagun and now I believe it."

Parker whirled. A dapper, slender man of about five feet six or seven, stood at the bar with one elbow resting on it. It was Sheriff Grigsby. His free hand held a glass of whiskey.

"All right, Morland," Grigsby said. "Get out of town; this gets around every tough bird in Gunsight'll take a crack at you. Beat it . . . I'm Hal Grigsby, the sheriff. Met you last night at the fun."

"It wasn't fun," said Parker.

"Not for the boys, you mean. I've been lookin' for you, Smith. How'd you like to be my deputy? Seventy-five a month."

"The marshal's job pays more than that."

"So it does – in salary. I didn't finish. Seventy-five a month and twenty per cent. This is a fee office; it's good for forty thousand a year. That's eight thousand for you, plus your seventy-five a month. All you've got to do is take orders."

Parker looked steadily at the dapper little man. "Whose orders?"

"Just mine."

"And who do you get yours from?"

"Ah, somebody's been talkin' to you.

Never mind. The job still holds."

"What duties would I have?"

"The usual deputy's duties. You'd serve papers, help collect taxes and make arrests; in the county, of course. Not in the towns."

"The arrests would have to be made on your orders?"

"Right!"

"I'll take the job, then – if your first order is to arrest Fletch Hobbs, Johnny Shade and Kearney Spence."

"What for? They were acquitted last night by Judge Anderson."

"How about Andrew Spence then?"

"On what charge?"

"Murdering Judge Megan."

"You can prove that?"

"He left the jail after threatening Judge Megan. A minute later Megan was blasted from the street."

"You have witnesses who saw it?"

"No," said Parker. "Shall we just forget it?"

"I didn't think you'd take the job," said Sheriff Grigsby. "But it was worth trying. You came in on the stage with George Layton, I understand." He smiled disarmingly, then shot out: "How much is he paying you?"

"For what?"

"For your job! Layton's been up in Dodge. Dodge is famous for two things, because it's trail's end and because it's got more fancy revolver men than any other town in this country. Layton and Spence busted their partnership in Dodge. Spence comes back with Dave Temple and Layton brings you."

"The idea's interesting," said Parker. "There's only one thing wrong with it – it's full of holes. If you'll check up you'll discover that I boarded the stage just the other side of Bisbee, and Layton got on at Brownsville."

"Thats fair enough. He sent you overland down the trail."

"Well," said Parker, "let it ride at that."

"Fine, but d'you mind if I remind you of something? That I'm the sheriff of this county? So if you kill Dave

Temple, make sure you've got witnesses who see you do it – in self-defense. And," Grigsby coughed gently, "the self-defense doesn't go if you shoot Andy Spence. He's not a gunslinger."

Parker smiled thinly and turned his back on the sheriff. After a moment he heard him walk off. Then he ordered a glass of beer. The bartender put it before him and leaned across the boards.

"Don't make a mistake, Smith," he whispered; "Grigsby's the smartest of them all."

"I didn't underestimate him. Nice town, Gunsight. Only trouble is that I can't get a room."

"If you can sleep with this racket here, we've got one upstairs. Two dollars a day. Top of the stairs, last room on the left."

"I'll take it, sight unseen"

"Well, it ain't much to look at, but it's got a bed . . . and a lock. My room's right across from yours. My name's Matt Royce."

Parker went up to the room and found

that it was a mere cubbyhole, about five feet by eight feet in size. Its only furniture consisted of a brass bedstead on which was a mattress stuffed with straw. There was a blanket on top of the mattress. He had not slept well the night before and, throwing himself down on the bed, he was soon fast asleep.

It was two o'clock when he awakened. He could hear activity in the saloon below and saw that it was well patronized when he went through it a few minutes later. He crossed the street to Ethel Halsted's restaurant and found her busy with a Chinese waiter, waiting on eight or ten customers.

She flashed him a smile, however, and when she came to take his order said in a low tone: "You're not leaving, then?"

"Not today."

"Going to the dance? Johnny Shade was in. *He's* going."

Parker hadn't even heard about the dance. But Ethel's warning got him to thinking about it. As he paid for his meal he asked, "Are you going to the dance?"

"Of course; everybody's going."

Leaving the restaurant, Parker strolled across the street to the office of *The Gunsight Target.* Dick Pendleton was in shirt sleeves, his face smudged with ink. He was glancing at a newspaper still damp.

"Parker!" he exclaimed. "Just the man I want to see. *The Target* hit the street ten minutes ago and in a little while we'll have some repercussions."

"Maybe you will at that," Parker admitted. He looked around the tiny office, separated from the printing plant in the rear by a corrugated sheet steel partition. A fowling piece stood in the corner, but otherwise he could see no other arms. "I met the sheriff," he said. "He just now offered me the job of deputy."

"Grigsby? I don't understand . . ."

"He had it all figured out that I'd refuse. He's got an idea that I'm a gunfighter from Dodge, hired by George Layton to kill Andrew Spence."

"But that's absurd. Layton told me

he'd never met you until yesterday."

"That's right. Grigsby said Spence had brought a man named Temple home with him. Dave Temple. Who is he?"

"A former buffalo hunter turned killer. There's a rumor that he used to ride with Harvey Dawson."

"That makes him a badman?"

Pendleton shrugged. "Every man in the West, handy with a gun, is rumored to be one of Harvey Dawson's men. Last week they said Harvey Dawson himself was here in Gunsight. The week before they had Billy the Kid here."

"From New Mexico?"

"Yes, Lincoln County. Billy's only nineteen years old, they say, but he's supposed to have killed almost twenty men. Personally, we've got men here in Gunsight worse than either Billy or Harvey Dawson. Johnny Shade, Fletch Hobbs."

"Thats me!" said a voice at the door. "Hello, Smith. How're you today?"

"Fine. I was just subscribing to *The Gunsight Target.*"

"Better get your money back, Smith. *The Target* may not come out again. Mr. Pendleton, I just heard some of the boys up the street talking about it. They don't like some of the things you said about them."

Parker, watching Pendleton, saw that the young publisher's face was taut. But Pendleton had sand. He said: "I told the truth, as I saw it. Are you objecting personally?"

"Yeah, sure; look!" Hobbs unfolded a copy of *The Target* that he had brought with him. "It says here: 'The worst of these so-called bad men is Fletcher Hobb.' . . . I don't like to see my name misspelled, Mr. Pendleton. There's an 's' on the end of it. Would you make it a point to see that the 's' is on the next time?"

Pendleton stared at Hobbs. "Are you serious? Is that all you object to?"

"Uh-huh. You see, Johnny Shade's an educated fellow. He called this to my attention and said that newspaper people often misspell names on purpose, because it makes people sore to have their names misspelled. You didn't do it on purpose, did you?"

"No. It was a typographical error."

"Typo-typographical error? Is that what you call it? Hmm, must spring that one on Johnny. By the way, if he comes here by himself don't pay no attention. Johnny's a little playful at times. If he starts shootin' up the place, you'll know he's only jokin' and not really meaning it at all. Afternoon, gents!"

"Whew!" exhaled Pendleton, after Hobbs had gone.

"I think perhaps I underestimated Hobbs," said Parker. "The man's more dangerous than I thought, because he's got a sense of humor. Johnny Shade hasn't. You don't carry a gun, do you, Mr. Pendleton?"

"No, I wouldn't know how to use it if I did."

"Maybe you better learn. Where do you sleep?"

"There are a couple of cots in back. Mike Finnegan, my printer, and I both sleep there."

"Good. If I were you I'd get some buckshot for that bird gun and anyone fools around the door at night, I'd let fly with the buckshot."

10

LEAVING the newspaper office, Parker walked to the western edge of Gunsight. Four hundred yards away, just south of the road, was a huddle of corrugated sheet iron buildings. Tall chimneys rose from a couple of the buildings and smoke was pouring from them. He went towards the buildings, but just as he was able to read a sign, *Gunsight Mining Corporation,* a man with a rifle stepped out from one of the buildings and yelled at him: "Private property, Mister. Keep away from here!"

Parker returned to the road and continued on for another half-mile. He counted seven different mines in that short journey, but did not try to approach any of them.

It was after four when he returned to Gunsight. He got a shave at the Elite

Barber Shop. As he came out he almost collided with Johnny Shade, a startlingly different Johnny Shade from the one he had encountered the day before.

Johnny had doffed his dirty linen coat and was wearing a suit of black broadcloth, his trousers tucked into a fine, stitched pair of cowboy boots. He wore a black Stetson, a spotless white shirt and a string bow tie. Parker conceded mentally that Johnny Shade was a handsome man.

"Getting ready for the dance?" Johnny asked pleasantly.

"I wasn't planning on it."

"Everybody'll be there. I'm taking my girl." He looked steadily at Parker, then nodded across the street. "Ethel Halsted."

Parker was surprised. Ethel Halsted had warned him against Johnny Shade and yet . . . well, he had only Johnny Shade's word for it. But Johnny was all slicked up.

Shade grinned at Parker. "No hard feelings – about last night?"

"For a half-hour I was the marshal," Parker said. "It was a job. Since I haven't got the job any more, what you do is no concern of mine . . . unless it's done to me."

"That's fair. Look, suppose we have a drink?"

"Beer's all I take."

"That's all I'm drinking today."

They went into the nearest saloon, which turned out to be called the Golden Nugget. It was smaller than the O. K. They sipped beer at the bar.

"You interest me, Smith," Shade said. "I can't make you out. Why'd you come to Gunsight?"

"Why did anyone come here? You, for example . . ."

"Oh, I've been here for several years. I was a cowboy on the L-S until I got tired of working. I'm from North Carolina, originally. My name wasn't Shade."

"No?"

"Uh-uh. Before the gold strike here every fourth man was named Smith." Shade chuckled "There were twelve

Smiths with Manny Higgins at one time."

"What're you driving at, Shade?"

"Nothing. Just my infernal curiosity. You're not a cowboy and I don't think you're a gambler, although you skinned Morland out of a few dollars today, I hear. Grigsby . . . "

"Grigsby thinks Layton hired me to do some work for him."

"Did he?"

"No. I never saw George Layton until yesterday . . . What kind of music will they have at this dance?"

The change of subject was so sudden that Johnny Shade grimaced. "All right, how about another beer?"

Parker agreed, but insisted on paying for the round. Johnny tossed off his drink, then signalled to the bartender, who brought out a bottle of whiskey. "Can't drink that much beer," he said.

He filled a two-ounce glass with the whiskey and drank it in two gulps. When he turned to Parker again, his eyes were shining.

"I think I'll have supper," Parker said.

"At Ethel's restaurant?"

"They serve good food."

"They? You mean Ethel." A note of challenge had come into Shade's voice. "Ethel needs the business, but don't forget what I told you – she's my girl!"

"All right, if she wants you – "

"I'm telling you, Smith. Don't crowd your luck too far."

Parker walked out abruptly. Shade had been cold sober when he had encountered him; the man had had two beers and one glass of whiskey and had become quarrelsome.

Parker wasn't afraid of Shade, but thought it just as well to avoid unnecessary trouble. So instead of going to Ethel Halsted's restaurant he returned to the O. K. Saloon and went to his room. He locked the door on the inside and went to sleep.

The din of a full saloon awakened him and he discovered that it was pitch dark in his room. He lay for a moment in the darkness, then, sighing wearily, got up and went downstairs. When he reached the lighted stairs he looked at his watch and discovered that it was a quarter to eight. He was hungry and went across to the restaurant. Matt Royce was the only customer in the place.

"Smith!" he exclaimed. "Figured you'd be at the dance by now. I just got off a while ago myself, so I'm grabbing a quick supper, then I figure to run over and see what's what. Come along?"

The Chinese came to take Parker's order. Ethel Halsted did not seem to be in the restaurant. He nodded. "I may look in. I haven't danced in four years."

"Good. Every female in the county'll be there, I guess. Lot of them been moving in. That's why I'm going. It's going to be a lot of fun. No drinking – inside – and all guns checked. I guess they can't prevent the men from going out to get a drink, but at least there won't be any gunplay and that's a relief. Too damn much of that stuff in this town. They ought to get in some of those tough Dodge City marshals who'd enforce an ordinance forbidding guns being carried in town . . . Mmm, I ought to learn to keep my mouth shut. You're from Dodge, aren't you?"

"No. I've been there, but never as long as I've been in Gunsight. Grigsby's mistaken."

"I thought so, when you didn't go with Layton to the capital."

"Layton's left town already?"

"Caught the six o'clock stage."

Parker looked again at his watch. It was eight o'clock. The stage was two hours to the west, too far to be caught even by a swift horse. He frowned.

"I'm not hungry. Shall we go to this dance?"

"You bet!"

The dance hall, if it could be called that, was at the east end of town. Actually it was an unfinished building that was to be the largest saloon in Gunsight. So far the floor had been built and the roof partially put on, but two of the four side walls still consisted of bare joists. A railing had, however, been hastily nailed around to keep the guests within the limits of the building or perhaps prevent nonpayers from entering.

Just inside the front door a man sat behind a table. Behind him was a long board into which nails had been driven. Guns of all types and descriptions hung from the nails, each with a little tag, on which the owner's name had been written.

"Two dollars and your shootin' iron, gents!"

Parker surrendered his gun and belt. Matt Royce was not armed. They passed into the dance hall, jammed with citizens of Gunsight. Benches had been built around three sides of the dance floor.

At the far, open end of the room was the orchestra, consisting of a violinist, a cellist, a Negro with a guitar and a chinless youth with a harmonica. They gave forth the weirdest music Parker had ever heard. But the dancers didn't mind.

They stamped, tugged and pushed about the floor with enthusiasm.

Almost the first person Parker saw was Jill Layton dancing with Kearney Spence. She did not see Parker, but there was a frown on her face that indicated she was not enjoying the dance with Kearney.

They passed and then he saw Ethel Halsted and Johnny Shade. Johnny's face was flushed and he was weaving drunkenly among the other dancers. Ethel was wearing a deep, wine-colored velvet dress. Parker's eyes went from Ethel to Jill, and then he guessed the answer to a riddle that had been in his mind ever since Ethel Halsted had let drop a remark the first time he had talked with her.

She'd told him the climate of Missouri hadn't agreed with her.

He'd seen the red spots in her cheeks in the restaurant and had laid it to the heat of the kitchen. He saw it now and compared it to the healthy complexion of Jill Layton and he knew that Ethel

Halsted was ill . . . a sickness that had required her to move to a hot, dry climate.

The music stopped and the dancers applauded vigorously, but the orchestra refused to play on so the floor began gradually to clear, making the outer fringe a solid jam of humanity. In the crush, Matt Royce, the bartender, was carried away from Parker. But his place was taken by a less welcome arrival.

Fletch Hobbs gripped Parker's elbow. "They make a swell couple, don't they? Johnny Shade and the Halsted girl."

"Shade's drunk."

"That's nothing new. He's always drunk. Sometimes he's drunk before breakfast. Whiskey makes him crab. I'm the only man who can handle him."

"Then why don't you take him away from the girl? Look!"

On the far side of the room, Ethel Halsted was backed up against a two-by-six. Johnny Shade was gripping her arms and Ethel was struggling to free herself.

Parker started to push free of the press around him. Fletch Hobbs clung to his elbow. “Wait a minute, Smith. No use to start a fight the condition he’s in. I’ll get him away.”

Both Parker and Hobbs broke through the fringe on to the dance floor. And then they saw that it was too late to get Johnny Shade away without a fight. A husky young blond fellow was just in the act of tearing Shade away from Ethel. As Parker started across the floor he saw Shade hit the blond in the face. The man took the blow smiling, then brought up a huge fist and clipped Shade on the jaw. The gunfighter sagged, but didn’t fall to the floor because the other man held him up.

Fletcher Hobbs shot past Jim Parker and swung his fist at the blond youth. The man, fortunately, saw the blow coming, let go of Shade and ducked. Hobb’s fist struck him a glancing blow on the shoulder.

Parker stepped in front of Hobbs. “Shade had that coming to him!”

Tight-lipped, Hobbs faced Parker. "Maybe he did, Smith, but Johnny's my pardner."

"He was annoying the young lady," the young blond cut in. "Where I come from, we don't let drunks maul women. I know who you are, Fletch Hobbs, but if you want to make anything of it – "

"Tomorrow Johnny Shade'll do something about it," snapped Hobbs in a menacing voice.

Sheriff Grigsby materialized out of the crowd. "What's the trouble here, Fletch?"

"No trouble! Johnny tripped and hurt himself. Help me take him out."

Grigsby looked sharply at Jim Parker, then shrugged and helped Hobbs with Johnny Shade.

"Thanks, mister," said the man who had slugged Shade.

"Thank *you,*" Ethel Halsted cut in. "And you, Mr. Smith."

"Smith? Say you're not the man who – "

"Yes," Ethel replied for Parker. "He's

the man who."

"I'm sure glad to meet you, Mr. Smith. My name's Mainwaring. I'm over at the Gunsight Mining Corporation. The whole shift was talking today how you . . ." He broke off. Parker had nodded to Ethel Halsted and she was smiling suddenly at young Mainwaring. The blond miner cleared his throat. "How about this next dance, Miss . . . ?"

"Ethel Halsted. I'd be glad to dance with you."

The orchestra started playing at that moment. The rush for the dance floor swirled Parker along the side lines and brought him up less than five feet from Jill Layton, who was sitting – with Mrs. Layton, a middle-aged man with a spade-shaped beard on one side of them and Dick Pendleton, the publisher, on the other. Pendleton was getting to his feet. He reached for Jill Layton's hand, but paused when he saw Parker.

"Mr. Smith! I've been looking for you . . . Uh, Miss Layton, have you met . . . Oh, of course, you came in on the stage together. I'm getting confused."

That was obvious enough. Pendleton was blushing and stammering like a schoolboy. Jill Layton got to her feet. "How do you do, Mr. Smith? Shall we dance, Dick?"

Jill Layton was wearing a green velvet evening gown. Her hair was brushed until it was shiny and golden. She wore a faint perfume that wafted to Parker's nostrils as she brushed past him.

She had met Pendleton only that day and she called him Dick. She had met Parker weeks ago, and called him Mister. Of course; she knew his identity.

She knew that he was Jim Parker of Missouri.

"Mr. Smith!" a voice said behind him.

He whirled, looked at the middle-aged woman. She smiled at him. "I'm Mrs. Layton," she said. "My husband was telling me about you. This is Mr. Kennard, Gunsight's leading attorney."

"You honor me, Mrs. Layton," said Kennard. He got up and shook hands with Parker. "How do you do, sir. George Layton told me about you. Er, as a matter of fact, I also read about the affair in the newspaper. Deplorable!"

"What's deplorable, Mr. Kennard?" Jennie Layton asked, smiling. "The way a member of your profession construed the law?"

"Harrump!" said Mr. Kennard. "I would not criticize a colleague. I was referring to the entire Gunsight situation. Squatters, all of these people. The land belongs to your husband, Mrs. Layton. I advised immediate suit against all of them."

Parker was standing before them, embarrassed. Mrs. Layton said: "What do you think of Gunsight, Mr. Smith?"

"It's a boom town, Mrs. Layton. I . . . they all seem to settle down after a while."

"That's what I've heard. I understand Abilene and Dodge City . . . and Cheyenne were all like this for a time. I believe my daughter said she met you . . . in Dodge City or near by . . . ."

Parker stiffened. Jill Layton had told her mother.

He said, evenly, "Your daughter did me a service, ma'am."

"And you did one for her . . . and for my husband, yesterday. By the way, he only knows about yesterday."

Parker relaxed a little. "Thank you, Mrs. Layton." He started to turn away and saw Kearney Spence bearing down on him.

"Smith," Spence said.

Parker moved toward him and said in a voice so low that Mrs. Layton would not be able to hear, "I don't think I care to talk to you, Spence. I might remember something."

"You don't have to talk to me," Kearney Spence said, angrily. "But there's a man outside wants to talk to you. His name is Ben Walker."

"Ben Walker?"

"Yes. He wants to talk to you about his brother."

Well, it had come. All day he had marked time, feeling that he was sitting on a keg of gunpowder which might explode at any minute. And now the match was lit.

He worked his way slowly around the edge of the dance floor. When he reached the door he looked toward the rack where his gun was hanging.

A dirty, unshaven man with bloodshot eyes stood in front of the table behind which sat the keeper of the guns. He wore a ragged coat; the left sleeve of it hung limp and the arm was obviously in a sling.

"Smith," the man said, "come outside."

Parker saw no gun dangling beneath Ben Walker's coat. He might have concealed one on his person, but he was wounded. Parker had his derringer in his vest pocket.

He said: "You're making trouble for yourself, Walker."

"Come outside," Walker said thickly. "Come outside and I'll bash in your brains with my one good hand."

Walker backed out of the door and Parker followed. The wounded bandit began fumbling with the buttons of his coat and Parker spoke sharply.

"Don't, Walker. I'll kill you if you reach for a gun."

Walker's coat opened and revealed – not a bandaged left hand, but a fist already holding a cocked Frontier Model.

Parker leaped to the side, his hand whipping to his vest pocket for the derringer. His fingers touched it even as the gun in Walker's hand thundered.

A red-hot knife blade tore through Parker's left shoulder and the force of the bullet spun him completely around. His startled eyes saw the mad, blazing face of Johnny Shade.

"Smith!" Shade cried. "This is your finish!"

Parker fell to his knees, stabbing up with the derringer. He pressed the trigger and knew from the slap against his palm that the gun exploded. But he didn't see the results of the shot. He didn't see, because the sky seemed to fall down on him. A roaring filled his ears.

11

JIM PARKER knew very little about the days that followed. He was unconscious most of the time. When he was awake his vision was blurred and his brain felt almost as numb as his body. He knew that he traveled for a long time in a wagon and then once he awakened to find himself in a room in which the walls were all white. But that couldn't be because he had never been in a room with white walls in all his life. And he hadn't been in a bed with clean, white sheets in months and months.

Yet he awoke again in the white room. He was awake for some minutes during which both a man and a woman in white uniforms came and looked down on him. He realized that he was in a hospital room, but he went to sleep once more and slept for a long time.

The next time his eyes opened, the

nurse was smiling at him. "You'll be all right," she said. "A few weeks' rest, that's all you'll need."

"Where am I?" Parker asked.

"Tucson. You've been here twelve days."

"Twelve days! How long before . . ."

"Five. It's seventeen days altogether since you were shot. I don't mind admitting that Dr. Plumb didn't expect you to pull through at first. You had three bullets in you."

Parker was silent for a few moments. Then he asked: "And the man . . . the men who . . ."

"You'd better go to sleep again," the nurse said, evasively. "The more rest, the sooner you'll be on your feet."

It was three more days before he learned the truth and then he got it by bribing an orderly to bring him some old Tucson newspapers.

Walker was dead. He was the brother of an outlaw Smith had killed two days previously and had obviously sought out Smith to revenge his brother. A bystander named John Shade had been slightly wounded in the arm. Johnny Shade, an innocent bystander . . .

Then Parker saw the real story in the newspaper, the one with the headline all the way across the paper. It read:

GEORGE LAYTON KILLED IN STAGE HOLDUP

Prominent Cattleman Murdered As He Travels to Tucson To Petition Governor

George Layton, prominent cattleman, was shot and killed last night during a stage holdup which occurred twelve miles west of the boom town of Gunsight. Layton, with his partner, Andrew Spence, owned the largest cattle ranch in the territory of Arizona. Recently, the two men dissolved their partnership, dividing their land and holdings. Layton acquired the entire eastern half of Gunsight Valley, in which section are located the valuable mines and the entire townsite of Gunsight. It is understood that Layton, who recently returned from a trip to Kansas, was on his way to petition Governor Nolting to enjoin the mine owners and business men of Gunsight from stripping the wealth off the property he claims.

According to the testimony of the stage driver, the express messenger and two fellow passengers, the stage bearing Layton was stopped by two masked men, twelve miles out of Gunsight. The passengers were lined up beside the stage and search of their persons was begun, when Layton suddenly reached for his revolver. One of the bandits shot him through the head, and it was believed that he was instantly killed. The bandits then proceeded with their work and made good their escape.

Sheriff Harold Grigsby of Oro Grande County is said to be hot on the trail of the murderers and it is believed that an arrest is imminent.

Layton is survived by his widow, Jennie Layton, and one daughter, Jill.

The stage had left Gunsight at six

o'clock. Layton had probably been killed before eight. He was already dead when Parker had seen Jill Layton and her mother at the dance in Gunsight. They hadn't known at that time, of course.

Parker re-read the item. It was a lie. Parker had been on a stage with Layton. The cattleman had carried a fat wallet and had passed it to a bandit. He would not resist in a subsequent, similar situation. No, the holdup had been planned for one purpose only – to kill George Layton.

Someone had known his reason for journeying to the territorial capital.

Parker sent for more newspapers. There was much mention of the Layton murder, but one item was conspicuous by its absence. The arrest of the murderers.

A few days after Layton had been buried, Parker learned that B. P. Killian had been appointed judge for the Gunsight district, and a day later *The Gunsight Target* reported the appointment of Joe Pelkey as town marshal at a salary of one hundred and fifty dollars a month.

Parker spent hours reading the Tucson papers. There was a daily Gunsight bulletin reporting the progress of the boom town. Gold was seldom discussed any more; the big talk was silver. One of the mines had opened up a vein forty-five feet wide. The boom was reaching its height and Gunsight boasted a population in excess of five thousand.

It averaged better than one violent death per day.

On the nineteenth day of his admission to the Tucson Hospital Jim Parker walked to the shaded veranda with the assistance of an orderly.

He sat there for hours, looking toward the east. He did a lot of thinking. Much of it had to do with his past life and very little of it was pleasant.

He thought about a man who had come to the Parker home in Missouri, ten years ago. It was night and the man was wounded. His father knew the man and took him in. They washed his wound and gave him shelter for days and then one night the man went quietly away.

Then Jim Parker's father said, "That man was Harvey Dawson. I served with him in the war, when he was only a boy not much older than you are now, Jim. For that reason I'll always help him. But never mention his name to anyone outside of this house."

Jim Parker didn't mention the name, but he was sixteen. He could read and he could listen. But he couldn't do either without coming across the name of Harvey Dawson. Dawson had held up another bank; he had robbed the Union Pacific. He had outwitted a posse, made fools of Colonel Bligh and Captain Street.

Years later, Harvey Dawson came again to the Parker home, but Parker, Senior, was no longer there. Young Jim Parker rode away with Harvey Dawson.

It had been different than he'd expected. Harvey Dawson had been at it too long.

And now Jim Parker sat in the hot Arizona sun. Harvey Dawson was fifteen hundred miles away, skulking perhaps in the brush with a posse searching for him.

The nurse came out to the veranda. "You'll be as good as new in a couple of weeks," she said.

He looked at her thoughtfully. "How did I get here to the hospital from Gunsight?"

"You were brought in a wagon. I understand the doctors in Gunsight gave you up so your friends had you brought here."

"My friends?"

"Of course. They – they guaranteed the bill."

"What are their names?"

"I wouldn't know. The office has that information."

"Can you find out?"

The nurse went off. When she returned her face was puckered. "They don't know. Two men brought you in a wagon, but refused to give any names. They left five hundred dollars in greenbacks."

With George Layton dead, who in Gunsight would pay five hundred dollars to keep him alive?

12

THE things that happened that night crushed the Layton women. They were at the dance when the gun fight between Jim Parker and Walker and Johnny Shade took place. The dance continued but Jill and her mother went home. Dick Pendleton and Arch Cummings rode with them.

They were less than a hundred yards from the ranch house when a galloping rider overtook them.

"Mrs. Layton," he panted. "I got some bad news to tell you. It came right after you left town. Mr. Layton . . . he's been . . . shot . . . "

Jill Layton fainted. When she revived she was in her bed at the ranch house and her mother was seated in a rocking chair beside the bed. She was rocking steadily. Her eyes were dry, but they were dull.

She did not cry, two days later, when they buried George Layton on top of the hill behind the ranch house. But afterwards, she said to Jill. "I suppose we ought to leave this country."

"No, Mother," Jill said, "we can't. I don't think Father would like it."

"I'm glad to hear you say that. I've been here thirteen years," Jennie Layton said. "I never liked this country. I stayed because of your father. I guess I can stay a little while longer."

Later that day, Arch Cummings came to Jill where she was sitting on the veranda. "Miss Jill," he said, "the boys asked me to talk to you. I mean, they asked me to find out . . . what you figure on doing?"

"I don't know, Arch," Jill said. "Is it necessary to make a decision?"

"The boys want to know. You see they figure to do something about what happened . . . "

"But they don't know who did it."

"They figure Andy Spence might know."

"No," said Jill, "they couldn't prove that."

"They wasn't figurin' on provin' it."

Jill shook her head. "Tell the boys – no. I don't think Dad would want it that way."

"You're dad had to fight all the time he lived here."

"But he fought square. And that's the way he'd want us to continue the fight."

Arch Cummings rubbed his chin and thought a while. "All right, if you say so, Miss Jill. But there ain't much fair fightin' goin' on around Gunsight. We thought for a while that Smith fellow they made marshal . . . but he's cashin' in his chips."

"He's dying?"

"He's got three bullets in him. Doc Wilson doesn't want to operate. Says he ought to go to the hospital in Tucson."

"Then why don't they take him there?"

"Cost money. And who'll take him? Nobody much is interested in Jim Smith around here. Your dad was counting on Smith to help clean up Gunsight . . ."

"Take him to Tucson, Arch," Jill said. "Get a couple the men and take him there. I'll get the money. But Smith isn't to know who's paying for it. Understand?"

Dick Pendleton helped during the coming days. Seldom a day that he didn't ride out to the ranch and remain for a couple of hours. His quiet strength helped Jill Layton. She didn't want to talk and she didn't listen to everything he said; her attention wandered often. But Pendleton didn't mind.

It was ten days before Kearney Spence rode over. He was sober and his eyes were clear. "You know how Dad and I feel, Jill," he said. "I haven't come over because I thought you'd prefer to be alone a while, but . . ."

"Thanks, Kearney. You're looking well."

He grinned wryly. "I'm on the water wagon. Dad made me foreman of the ranch and I'm working hard, for a change. Dad said to ask if there was anything you wanted; men to help you on the ranch or anything."

"I don't think there's anything we want, Kearney. But thanks, just the same."

Two days later Andrew Spence came over. He talked to Jennie Layton. "Maybe it was a mistake, George and I splitting the ranch. Of course we didn't know at the time about this strike, but since it's here, well, we'd both been better off to stick together and fight the thing through."

"We're not fighting anything any more, Andrew," said Mrs. Layton.

"You mean you want to give up? It *is* a pretty big job for a woman."

"Two women, Andrew."

"Jill? Of course. But, ah, well, it may work out. You know George and I used to talk about Jill and Kearney . . . "

"That's up to them. Right now Jill isn't thinking of that."

Andrew Spence frowned. "That's the trouble. Things are moving at a terrific pace in Gunsight Valley. Have you been missing any stock lately?"

"Arch Cummings hasn't said anything about it."

"Probably doesn't want to worry you. I've lost several hundred head. The Mexican rustlers below the river are taking advantage of the situation here. It's becoming worse day by day. I find it hard to get enough good men and I know most of your men have deserted to work in the mines. Too bad we couldn't have foreseen this and delayed splitting up our partnership. I don't like to talk about all this at a time like this, Jennie, but I think you should seriously consider merging our holdings once more. Be better for both of us."

"It undoubtedly would be, Andrew, but with George gone, I don't like to think of doing *anything* right now."

"I know, but give it some thought, Jennie, will you? I'll ride over again in a few days."

When he had gone, Mrs. Layton sent for Arch Cummings. "Are we losing any stock, Arch?"

"Spence told you? Yes, Mrs. Layton,

we're losing stock. A lot of it. It's Manuel Higgins. He used to run stock from Mexico up here, but now there's a good market right in Gunsight and Bisbee and the railhead at Deming. Yes, we're losing stock, Mrs. Layton."

"And you're sure it's this Higgins?"

Cummings shrugged. "Higgins' men. He's got a hundred on both sides of the river. The riffraff from both countries, fugitives, outlaws. Higgins is their boss. When we had plenty men here they left us alone, but now – "

"Hire more men."

"They're hard to get."

"Pay more money."

"I'll try." Cummings' eyes clouded. "It ain't so much a question of money. Uh, Andy Spence's been able to hire quite a few men lately, but they . . . I'll give it to you straight, Mrs. Layton, they think this is the losing side."

"You mean we're sided against Spence?"

"I mean," Cummings said, slowly, "Higgins and Spence never have been very mad at each other."

"But he just told me he's lost a lot of stock!"

"He *told* you he lost stock."

"Hasn't he?"

Cummings shrugged "Spence's riders ain't been encouragin' us to ride through their herds. I don't know."

Mrs. Layton was silent a moment. "How much stock have we lost?"

"Hard to say; four-five hundred head. Maybe more."

"Thats too many. We can't go on losing like that. Arch, tell me something. What this ranch needs is a strong man, isn't it?"

Cummings did not answer. Mrs. Layton sighed. "Hire those men, Arch. *Good* men, understand?"

"Yes, Mrs. Layton."

When Jill came into the house later, her mother said, "Jill, whatever became of Jim Parker? I haven't looked at a newspaper or anything. Did he . . ."

"No. They took him to the hospital in Tucson."

"Who took him?"

Jill flushed. "Some men. I asked Arch to have some of the men take him. They said he would die in Gunsight."

"And he's recovering now?"

"I haven't heard. I haven't even thought of him, since – "

"I know, Jill. How would you like to take a trip to Tucson?"

"What? Why?"

"To see how Jim Parker's coming along."'

Jill exclaimed, "But why, Mother?"

"Because we need him. Sit down, Jill, and let me tell you about some things I've learned."

Mrs. Layton did not mince words. She not only related to Jill all that Andrew Spence had said – and hinted at – but added Arch Cummings' own remarks. She finished: "We need a strong man as badly as Gunsight needs a marshal. I think this Parker is the man."

"But he's an outlaw, Mother. I told you that he's Jim Parker, who rode with Harvey Dawson."

"That was fifteen hundred miles away

and a long time ago. I think Parker has changed."

"He's a killer!"

"Your father was killed," Mrs. Layton said bluntly. "He was murdered!"

13

TUCSON had a population of less than eight thousand, not a great deal more than Gunsight. But it was older and more firmly rooted. It had streets and frame houses. It had a hospital. It was somewhat quieter.

Jill Layton followed the nurse through its wide corridors out to the sun porch on which Jim Parker was sitting in a wheelchair. Her eyes went wide as she noted the pallor of his face. He had lost weight too.

She said, "I was in Tucson and they told me you were convalescing."

His eyes seemed to be glowing. "You're the only visitor I've had. You didn't have to come . . . "

"I wanted to come. You know – about Father?"

"I read about it in the papers. I'm sorry."

She nodded. "Mother and I are carrying on, because we know he would have wanted us to. But things are difficult. We need, that is, Mother suggested I talk to you about coming to work for us."

He stared at her. "But you know who I am. Jim Parker . . . "

Her chin came up a little. "Yes, I know you're Jim Parker. But the job needs a man like Jim Parker."

"Oh! You want me to get the man who killed your father? Yes, of course, Jim Parker is the man for such – "

"You're trying to misunderstand," Jill Layton said, hotly. "We want you to work on the ranch. Rustlers are stealing our cattle and – to put it bluntly – Mother said we need a strong man. She knows who you are. I told her."

Parker's gaze fell from her face. "Someone had me brought here, paid the hospital. Did you?"

Jill said, hastily, "This is the first time I've ever been in Tucson."

Parker reached to the floor and picked up a newspaper. "I've been keeping up with Gunsight. I hadn't thought of returning there, but a job's a job and, well, things don't look so good in Gunsight. How is the marshal, Joe Pelkey?"

"Dick Pendleton says he's a fairly good man. Then you'll take the job? We'll pay you well and – "

"And what?"

"Nothing, I guess. As you said, a job's a job."

"They say I can leave here in a couple of days, but look – I'd rather look things over before I come out in the open. I think it would be better not to say anything about me working for you. I wasn't in Gunsight very long, but I picked up a few things that make me wonder."

"You mean Manuel Higgins?"

"I was thinking of him. I'd like to know more about him."

"He's a rustler; everyone knows that. But no one's ever done anything about it. Mother says it would be hard to prove anything on him, because he operates on such a large scale on both sides of the Border and has so many men, he doesn't take part personally in the raids."

Parker nodded. "That's what I gathered, and I think I ought to learn something about him. I was thinking I might throw in with him for a little while . . ."

"But wouldn't that be dangerous?"

"The streets of Gunsight are dangerous," Parker said evenly. "Of course I may not be able to get in with Higgins, but whatever I do, remember I'll be working for you."

"Very well. As for salary . . ."

"We can talk about that later."

So Jim Parker returned to Gunsight. He rode in on a huge sorrel that he had purchased in Tucson and before he had traversed halfway down Main Street, men were stopping to look at him. He had changed his shabby Prince Albert and broadcloth breeches for the costume of the range, wool shirt, levis, high-heeled boots and a flat-crowned Stetson. He wore a Frontier Model openly in holster that was tied down to his thigh with a leather thong.

He was pale and his face looked drawn, but he was obviously the man Gunsight had known as Jim Smith; the man who had killed the Walker brothers, wounded Johnny Shade and bluffed down Fletch Hobbs.

He rode steadily to the adobe hut that housed *The Gunsight Target* and there he dismounted from the sorrel and tied it to the hitch-rail. Dick Pendleton met him at he door of the newspaper office.

"Jim Smith! I'm glad you're back. Jill told me you were coming, but I didn't think you could make it so soon after — "

"I'm all right," said Parker. He entered the building. "What's the situation here?"

Pendleton shook his head. "Hell! We've got a marshal, man named Pelkey. He's rather good at handling minor hoodlums and drunken miners, but he's Grigsby's man."

"Grigsby's running Gunsight?"

Pendleton moistened his lips with his

tongue. "For Andrew Spence."

"Spence?"

"Spence is our Number One citizen."

"The new judge, Killian?"

"Surprisingly honest. Not the crusader that Megan was, but honest. The Spence faction don't like him."

"Who's on your side, Pendleton?"

"My side? I didn't know I had a side. But I know what you mean. The substantial citizens, who unfortunately have other things to do than play politics and clean up a boom town. Most of the storekeepers, the mine-owners, engineers and superintendents. The miners, who are bringing in their families. In short, the majority who are always ruled by a loud, aggressive minority."

Parker nodded thoughtfully. "I picked up a copy of your paper in Johnstown last night. It was pretty quiet."

Pendleton flushed. "It's had to be quiet. Everything I own is tied up in this business. My windows were broken and someone took a shot at me one night."

"I see."

"No, you don't, Smith. I'm ready to fight any time if I can be assured of even a small chance of winning. When it seemed like George Layton was backing me, well, I felt I had a chance."

Parker turned to the door, then stopped. "Jill Layton's taking it hard."

"Of course. You can't blame her, a girl her age, her father murdered . . . Still, if she'd broken down . . . ."

"She can't," Parker said. "Some people can't let go." Parker knew that.

He went outside and walked up the street. It was mid-morning and the restaurant would probably not be busy. He crossed to it and entered. The Chinese waiter was scrubbing the tables.

Ethel Halsted sat behind a newly installed counter, reading a newspaper. She looked up idly as Parker entered, then she dropped the paper and leaped to her feet.

"Jim Smith!"

"Hello."

The red spots in her cheeks had grown. Color flooded her entire face now. "I never expected to see you in Gunsight again."

"How is Johnny Shade?"

"Johnny . . . what do you mean?" But she did know what he meant and said so. "You're wrong about Johnny Shade and me. I went with him to that dance because it was easier to go than to refuse. There's nothing between Johnny and myself and there never will be. I know that Johnny is a . . . killer."

"I'm going to kill him," Parker said, simply.

Her eyes widened. "Why? Oh, I know that he was in that plot to kill you, but if you kill him now, it'll be murder."

"George Layton was murdered."

"But Johnny didn't do that. He couldn't have, because he was here in Gunsight when it happened."

"*I* know that," said Parker.

"Of course. Jim, I didn't think you'd come back to Gunsight."

"I didn't want to, but a man can't run

out on a job."

"A job?"

He shrugged. "Unfinished business."

A slight frown creased her forehead. "You're a strange man, Jim Smith. I can't make you out at all. You remind me of — well, someone I never met, but of whom I heard a lot back home."

"Missouri? Well, I come from there, too."

"Yes, but you're not . . . I wonder . . ." A speculative look came into her eyes.

Parker changed the subject. "But you're still serving meals. How about the Number 1?"

"Coming right up."

Later, Parker mounted the big sorrel and rode southward, out of Gunsight. The valley opened up and he bore to the left. The grass was good, he noted, and the numerous cattle he saw were in good flesh. Gunsight Valley was rich in more than minerals.

After a while he topped a knoll and looked across a depression in which there were several acres of stunted cottonwoods.

He could see clear over the trees to a slope beyond, on which stood the ranch house and out-buildings of the Layton ranch. He was somewhat surprised by the size and number of the buildings and regarded the layout for several minutes.

Then he turned his horse toward the west and skirted the cottonwoods. He rode through cattle and after an hour or so climbed a hill on which stunted piñon trees grew, and came upon the Spence ranch. After seeing the Layton spread, Parker was impressed by the shoddiness of the Spence buildings. They were mostly adobe sheds in a rundown condition. Even the main house was built of red adobe bricks, without benefit of mortar or chinking.

As he approached, Andrew Spence came out of the house and stood in front of the veranda. Parker rode up to within a dozen feet, then leaned forward and rested his left forearm on the pommel of the saddle.

"Howdy, Mr. Spence," he said.

"You're Jim Smith. What do you

want here?"

"I'm looking for a job."

"What?"

"A man's got to eat and I wasn't cut out for digging."

"You've got a lot of nerve coming here."

"Where else could I go? There're only the two ranches around here."

"Well, why not try the Layton ranch?"

Parker put his tongue in his cheek. "The job might not last."

"Eh? What do you mean?"

"This is a hard country. Takes a man to run a ranch, a hard man."

Spence regarded Parker thoughtfully for a moment. Then he shook his head. "If you'd come to me when you first got to Gunsight, I would have put you on. But after what you did to Kearney . . . "

"I didn't know him."

"But you knew Fletch Hobbs and Johnny Shade."

"Uh-uh. Well, sorry you haven't got a job. I'll be riding along."

"Wait a minute. Why'd you come back

from Tucson? To kill Johnny Shade?"

Parker shrugged. "If he forces it."

"You're very sure of yourself, Smith. Now that you know how tough he is, what makes you think you can down Shade?"

"I don't know if I can."

"But you're not afraid of him? Even after he shot you up?"

"There was a fellow helping him."

"Yeah. Yeah, sure. I don't get you, Smith. Where are you from?"

"I didn't think they asked that question, down here."

"They don't as a rule. But I'm damn curious. Johnny Shade would be tough anywhere. I've got a man here, Dave Temple, and he wouldn't pick a fight with Johnny Shade when Johnny's liquored up. Why don't you look up Manuel Higgins? I hear he's in Gunsight. He's got a lot of boys along the river."

"What do they do there – fish?"

"Not in the Rio Grande; it's about two inches deep in most places."

"I see. Maybe I'll run into Higgins in

Gunsight."

Parker turned his horse away. As he did he looked toward one of the bunkhouses and saw a squat, cruel-faced man standing in the doorway. From the evil look the man gave him, Parker guessed that he was Dave Temple. And he was right in his guess.

He rode slowly back to Gunsight, arriving there shortly after the change of shifts in the mines. The town was a solid mass of moving humanity, and he had difficulty in finding a place at the hitch-rail in front of the O. K. Saloon & Dance Hall. When he finally tied his horse and entered the place he discovered that it was doing a thriving business.

There were six bartenders behind the bar. Matt Royce stood at the end, wearing a silk shirt with arm bands, but minus the white apron.

He whistled when he saw Jim Parker, but instantly a grimace crossed his face. "Mr. Smith! I wasn't expectin' you back in Gunsight."

"I wasn't expecting to come back, two weeks ago. Business has picked up."

"Sure," said Royce. "And I'd be gettin' rich if the drunks didn't break up the mirrors and furniture every other day. What this town needs is a good marshal and about six policemen . . . What is it, Zeke?" The last to a colored roustabout, who had come up.

The swamper rolled his eyes and looked at Parker, then at Matt Royce. "Gen'men over there says, would this gen'man come talk to them?"

Parker turned and searched the saloon. "Where?"

"Over dere," said the darky, pointing.

There were two men at the table, one a dapper, swarthy man of about forty and the other – the other was Captain Street of the Bligh International Detective Agency.

Parker walked slowly over to the table. When he was still several feet away, Captain Street greeted him. "Hello, Mr. Smith. Nice to see you again. You remember me – Captain Purdy of

Johnson County?"

"Of course," said Parker. "How are you, Captain Purdy?"

"Couldn't be better. I'd like you to meet my friend, Mr. Manuel Higgins!"

14

PARKER'S eyes went quickly to the face of the dapper man. Higgins was dressed in an expensive suit of black serge and wore a rakish derby hat. He smiled at Parker, showing white teeth, and extended a hand on which were flashing a couple of diamond rings.

"I've been wanting to meet you, Mr. Smith," Higgins said. "Won't you join us in a drink?"

"I'll have a glass of beer," said Parker. He sat down. "Been in Gunsight long, Captain Purdy?"

"Mm, no. I was in Tucson for a couple of days. I'm interested in cattle. Mr. Higgins is one of our largest cattlemen, I understand, with herds on both sides of the Border."

Higgins winked. "I'm cattle poor, Captain. I've got too many and not enough money. Takes a lot to meet my payroll."

"I'm sorry to hear that, Mr. Higgins," said Parker. "I was planning to ask you for a job. Andrew Spence suggested I do so."

"Spence?" Higgins looked thoughtfully at Parker. "You asked him for a job?"

"Yes. He didn't want – he didn't have any openings."

"I can understand that."

Captain Street smiled pleasantly. "I can recommend Mr. Smith very highly. He'd make an excellent employee for your southern ranch."

"My *segundo* has already recommended Mr. Smith," said Higgins. "He spoke very highly of your ability – Fletcher Hobbs."

Parker arched his eyebrows, then shifted to Captain Street, now calling himself Captain Purdy. "How are things in Missouri, Captain?" he asked bluntly.

"Oh, quiet. Very quiet. Our best business men have emigrated to the Southwest, where things are humming."

Manuel Higgins pulled out a hunting

case watch. "I've a little appointment up the street. Will you be here for a while, Mr. Smith? I'd like to talk to you some more."

"I'll be here."

"Good: I'll see you in about a half-hour, then. You, too, I trust, Captain Purdy."

He got up and began working his way through the crowd toward the door. When he was out of earshot, Captain Street said, "Well, Jim, I almost lost you."

"You figure on arresting me?"

Captain Street shook his head quickly. "In Gunsight? No. As a matter of fact, I came to Arizona on an entirely different matter. Then I heard some stories about a man named Smith who had been marshal here for an hour or so and I became interested. I went to Tucson, but you'd already left. I really came here, however, because of Higgins."

"Do you know who he is?"

"Oh, yes! I arrested him once, back in '66, but he hired some good attorneys and got off. He did, however, leave Illinois after that. He came out here and made good. So well, in fact, that the government became interested in him. Because of his peculiar methods of business, I don't exactly see what the government can do about him. There's no question of Higgins being a rustler, but all his thieving is done in Mexico and the Mexican government is peculiarly apathetic about the entire matter. Smuggling, yes, but how many men can we put on the Border to prevent Higgins from driving a herd across and if we caught twenty rustlers running cattle across, what good would that do, as far as Higgins is concerned? We couldn't catch him. So . . . Where's Harvey Dawson, Jim?"

"There's no one by that name around here that I know of."

"Don't! You're Jim Parker and I know it."

"Suppose I am?"

"Nothing – now. Perhaps I could get you extradited, but frankly, would it be worth it? You were arrested in Nebraska on suspicion. On the identification of two people, one of whom has died and the other disappeared. Very good – for you! That reduces the charge to breaking jail . . . and if there's no other charge against you that one would collapse."

Jim Parker stared at Captain Street. "I don't get it. Then, why chase me to helangone?"

"I'm not chasing you. I'm here because of Higgins."

"Does he know who you are?"

"Of course. But he doesn't know *you.* Jim, I wonder if you'd be interested in a proposition?"

"I don't think so."

"You haven't heard what it is. How long did you ride with Harvey and his gang?"

"I never admitted that I even knew him."

"I know you didn't, but give us credit for knowing some things. It couldn't have been more than one, at the most two holdups. There were three men at

Deerfield and Mazomanie; four at Rocky Bank. I've checked back on you . . . and I'd still like to make you the proposition. Colonel Bligh will approve it, I know. How would you like to work on our side?"

Parker inhaled sharply, but he made no reply.

Captain Street was watching him closely. "We'll get the Rocky Bank thing quashed . . . and anything else."

"In return for what?"

"You know what."

"I don't know as much as you think I do. I don't know where Harvey Dawson is at this moment, any more than you do."

Captain Street pursed his lips. "Perhaps not at this moment. But you know Harvey Dawson. You know his friends."

"No," Parker said, curtly.

"You've had a long time to think about it, Parker."

"No!"

Captain Street sighed. "How about this job with Higgins? Will you – I mean, would you be interested in making some money on the side? A lot of money?"

"You can say about anything to me, can't you, Captain Street?" Parker asked, coldly. "Because you know I'm Jim Parker."

Captain Street turned up the palms of both hands. "You'll lose, Jim Parker. The Bligh Agency has always won. We've had some hard cases, but we've always won. Look up our record, sometime."

"I know it by heart."

"Dawson told you?"

"I don't know Dawson."

"Very well, Parker. You're safe from me — now. But the Bligh Agency never quits. Always, somewhere a Bligh man is awake . . . and watching . . . Well, here comes Mr. Higgins back. And he's got a friend with him."

The "friend" was Johnny Shade. He looked sober, but his eyes were slitted and he walked like a cat behind Manuel Higgins.

"Smith," said Higgins, "you know

Johnny Shade? He's working for me these days."

"Hello, Johnny," Parker said in a level tone.

"Any time," Johnny said.

Parker nodded. "I came back, but there's no hurry, is there?"

"Time doesn't mean anything to me." Shade's lip curled. "Nor does anything else."

"That's fine," exclaimed Manuel Higgins. "Johnny, shake hands with Captain Purdy. He's really Captain Street of Colonel Bligh's Detective Agency – "

Johnny Shade's hand which had been extended instinctively, was jerked back. "Is that your idea of a joke, Manny?"

"Not at all. I ought to know Captain Street. He arrested me, back in '66, or was it '67?"

"'66. I've heard of you, Mr. Shade, and I hope to have the pleasure of doing the same for you some day."

Johnny Shade bared his teeth in a snarl. "Try it and you might go home with some airholes in you."

"I wouldn't like that," Captain Street said, humorlessly. He got up. "If you'll excuse me, gentlemen. Some telegrams to send, you know . . . "

He nodded curtly to Shade, smiled at Higgins and gave Parker a thoughtful glance. Then he moved away. Manuel Higgins seated himself at the table. "Smith," he said, "I can use you – if you'll answer one question."

Parker shook his head. "No questions."

Johnny Shade sneered. "Still cocky, eh?"

Higgins' face lost its good humor. "Shut up, Johnny! All right, Smith, you don't have to answer the question. I'll make it a straight statement. Your name is really Parker."

Parker did not reply. Higgins smiled thinly. "I get them all, sooner or later. I read the papers and I remember. That derringer you've been using so freely – Jim Parker of Missouri used to carry one."

"Jim Parker!" exclaimed Johnny Shade. "What the – "

"I said shut up, Johnny!"

"I'll be damned," breathed Johnny Shade. "No wonder!" There was a sudden look of respect in his eyes.

"I met Harvey a couple of times," Higgins went on. "Once in '66 and another time in '69. Where is he, these days?"

"Harvey who?"

Higgins pawed the air impatiently with his right hand. "Captain Street practically verified it. But he'll never extradite you on the charge he's got. Forget him. I can use you, if you're Jim Parker."

"Shout that name around here, Higgins," Parker said evenly, "and you can go to hell."

Higgins grunted. "I never tell names. This is between us."

"And Johnny Shade!"

Johnny Shade glowered. "Even if you are Jim Parker, I never yet met the man I was afraid of. Harvey Dawson . . ."

Manuel Higgins' hand flicked out suddenly and slapped Johnny Shade's face. "I told you to keep your mouth shut."

Johnny Shade kicked back his chair and his hands went into the pockets of his linen coat. "Reach for your hardware, Manny Higgins!"

Manuel Higgins placed his hands flat on the table. You'd never ride out of Gunsight, Johnny, and you know it. Take your hands out of your pockets."

Johnny Shade brought out his hands and there was a Frontier Model in each. "No man ever slapped me in the face and got away with it, Higgins. I don't give a damn who you are. Reach for your gun, or take it!"

"Johnny," said Parker. "Look!"

Johnny Shade's eyes flicked to Parker, who was sitting at the side of the table, partly turned away. The muzzle of a revolver was poked over the table edge. It was pointing directly at Shade. The latter would have had to swing his guns three feet to hit Parker.

That split second would not be enough. Not against Jim Parker of Missouri.

Shade's tongue came out and licked his lips. His eyes seemed to bulge, and for a moment Parker thought Shade was going to try it after all.

But Shade was too sober.

His guns were lowered slowly and finally went back into his pockets. He shot a last glance at Parker, then turned and headed for the door.

Higgins exhaled heavily and drew a handkerchief from his pocket and patted his forehead. "That was a close shave. Thanks, Parker."

"Smith!"

"Smith. Shade is kill-crazy. He would have shot me. Well, that washes him up."

Outside the saloon a gun banged, then again and again. Jim Parker got up quickly and went to the door. As he threw it open, the gun went off once more and a voice screamed: "Yip-yip-yee-ow-ee!"

Johnny Shade, mounted on his horse, was in the middle of the street, in front of *The Target* office. He suddenly whirled his horse and shooting at the blue sky, galloped down the street.

Parker went swiftly to *The Target* office. As he approached he saw the shattered glass on the ground. Dick Pendleton came out, his face taut.

"I suppose I should have killed him," he said to Parker.

"He shot out your windows?"

"Yes, the drunken fool. I should have let him have it with the shotgun, but – "

"You'd have dreamed about it, Pendleton. Forget him."

"Did you dream – " Pendleton began, then winced. "Sorry."

Manuel Higgins came up. "Johnny Shade do that, Mr. Pendleton?"

Pendleton started to say something to Higgins, then his lips twitched and he turned and strode into his building. Higgins laughed shortly. "I don't think our editor likes me. Well, Smith, you want that job?"

"I'd like to try it."

"Good! Is your horse around?"

"In front of the O. K. Saloon."

15

HIGGINS had a tremendous red horse. Parker, who knew horses, regarded it with admiration. They rode side by side out of Gunsight, cutting down the valley in a direction that would take them close by the Layton ranch.

Higgins talked as they rode. "You should have been here thirteen years ago, Smith. Only people around here then were Apaches and fellows on the dodge, who were tougher than the Apaches. You ran like hell from the Apaches to save your hair and when your horse was winded you'd run smack into some fellow who'd shoot you for your horse."

"You seemed to have survived all that," Parker pointed out.

Higgins chuckled. "I did. But now I'm not too keen on Captain Street nosing around down here. Not that I'm afraid of him, but the Bligh outfit do a lot of work for the government and you can't tell what the government's apt to do to a fellow. This country's getting too civilized."

"Gunsight isn't very civilized," Parker said.

Higgins shrugged. "Not now. But how long will it last? If the mines don't peter out, the citizens are going to rise up one of these days like they did in California and up in Montana and organize a Vigilante committee. I figure to be gone by then, with my pile." He chuckled. "If people knew what I'm working on now, they wouldn't be sleeping so easy."

Parker shot a sideward glance at Higgins. "What's that?"

"Uh-uh, I'm not telling — yet! It ain't ripe, but it might be soon."

They were skirting the cottonwoods in the hollow before the Layton place. As they rode up the incline, Higgins nodded toward the ranch house. "I hate to rob a couple of women, but they ought to have the sense to pull out."

"Perhaps they feel they have to carry on."

"Why? George Layton's dead and nothing'll bring him back. Me, I never cared much for Layton."

"I gathered that . . . since he's dead."

"Eh? Not *me,* Parker."

"Smith! I suppose it was Andrew Spence?"

Higgins looked sharply at Parker. "What're you getting at?"

Parker coughed. "Ever see the Layton girl?"

"Yes, but what — Oh!"

"No," said Parker. "She's not my type. I like them a little hardier. But she's nice to look at and if we're doing any robbing, why don't we rob Andrew Spence?"

"You've got a down on Spence."

"I don't like his son. He led me out to Ben Walker and Johnny Shade."

"He was only getting even for what you did to him the day before. The kid's no good, but the old boy is quite a character. Uh, I may have a surprise for old Andy, at that. Do you know this is only nine miles from the Rio Grande?"

"What's on the other side?"

"Nothing but mesquite and rattlesnakes. And Matamoras, three hundred miles away. There used to be a lot of cattle on the south side of the river, but the Gringo rustlers thinned them out pretty well. S'tough!"

Manuel Higgins grinned.

Parker edged his horse closer to Higgins'. "Don't look right-away" he whispered, "but off to the left a couple of men are hiding, right over the ridge. One of them's got a rifle."

"Yeah," said Higgins. "I saw them." He put fingers to his mouth and blew a sharp, shrill whistle.

Two men wearing tremendous Mexican sombreros appeared. They were sunburned almost to the blackness of Apaches, but their features were those of white men.

"Hello, boys," Higgins called.

"Hello, boss," the men replied.

Higgins pointed at Parker. "Jim Smith. New man."

The men studied Smith, then nodded

and, turning, disappeared over the ridge.

"What do you think, Smith?" Higgins asked.

"Not bad; we're less than two miles from the Layton house. You've got them all the way through here?"

"Yep. Good thing to know. The boys don't like to be surprised . . . Let out your horse. It's getting late and I'd like to show you some things before it gets dark."

The country became rougher as they neared the river. Finally the valley narrowed down until it was a mere pass between forbidding peaks, too rugged to scale. The passage was not more than a hundred yards wide and a mile or so long. It opened abruptly at the south end of a sandy slope that ran down to the edge of the Rio Grande, a half-mile away.

Higgins turned his horse to the left, and Parker noted with surprise what seemed to be a village. At any rate there were fifteen or twenty buildings huddled together on the very banks of the Rio Grande. They were all built of adobe, in various stages of disintegration.

Higgins winked at Parker. "Kangaroo City. One big jump and you're across the river. There's no post-office and the stagecoach never comes either."

As they rode down upon Kangaroo City, men greeted Manuel Higgins. All were armed, many carrying two guns. Here and there a dark-skinned Mexican woman stood in a doorway.

There was a hitch-rail in front of one of the adobe huts, and here Higgins and Parker dismounted and tied their horses. They entered the building and Parker was astonished to find it fitted out as a saloon.

A Mexican with fierce mustachios was behind the bar. Leaning against it was Fletcher Hobbs. "Hi, Manny," he said. His eyes came to rest on Parker. "Long time no see, Smith."

The bartender spoke to Higgins in rapid Spanish. The latter exclaimed, "Where?"

"He come again," the bartender said in English. "Tonight."

Higgins' nostrils were flaring slightly and his eyes were glittering. "Have a drink, Parker?"

"Smith!"

"Parker?" asked Fletch Hobbs.

"He's Jim Parker – of Missouri," said Higgins.

Hobbs exclaimed, "Why didn't you say so in the first place? We wouldn't have had that trouble. Johnny – "

"Ah, Johnny!" cut in Higgins. "Johnny Shade's washed up, Fletch."

"Eh?"

"He pulled a gun on me and would have killed me, except that Par – Smith got the drop on him. Johnny's gone crazy. Last I saw of him he was shooting holes in the sky, like any drunken cowpuncher. Also he shot out the windows of *The Gunsight Target.*"

Fletch Hobbs scowled. "Johnny and me been pardners a long time."

"All right, but he's through."

"You mean that, Manuel?"

"Why?"

"Because I ride *with* Johnny."

Higgins' swarthy face became even darker. "Against me, Fletch?"

"Not against you, Manny, but with Johnny."

Higgins rubbed his chin. "Listen, I wasn't going to say anything, but there's a spic coming here . . . that's what Pedro was telling me. This fellow looks like a Mexican, but he's a Cuban. His name's *Señor* Ramon Gallegos."

"What's a Cuban got to do with me and Johnny Shade?"

"*Señor* Gallegos is a representative of the Captain-General of Cuba, who wants to buy fifty thousand beefs for that island. Those beefs are worth sixty dollars a head, delivered to Matamoras, where they'll get on boats and go to Cuba. But if *Señor* Gallegos buys all those beefs from Mexican cattlemen he won't make any profit for himself. And what's the use being a government official if you can't make any profit for yourself? So *Señor* Gallegos wants to buy those steers for thirty dollars a head. And he'll drive them to Matamoras himself."

Fletcher Hobbs' eyes were wide. "A million and a half dollars!"

"That's a lot of money, isn't it, Parker? The hell with the Smith."

Hobbs laughed. "Right across the river – and he'll lay it on the line?"

"In American currency; that much gold is too heavy."

"But fifty thousand beefs . . . "

Higgins nodded. "Its a lot of beef. However, I've been working on this for some time. I even talked to the captain of the *rurales.* For only ten thousand *pesos* he will be hunting bandits one hundred miles south of the Rio Grande, and only fifty miles away is a herd of fifteen thousand head of longhorns."

"That leaves thirty-five thousand."

Higgins put his tongue into his cheek.

Hobbs whistled. "Andy Spence has thirty thousand. And the Laytons – "

"Ten or more."

Hobbs shook his head. "What about Johnny?"

"Is he important?"

"I can handle Johnny, Manuel. If I'd

been with him today, nothing would have happened."

"All right, Fletch. I need you, and Johnny's got his uses. But if he ever pulls a gun on me again."

Fletch Hobbs squinted at Jim Parker. "Are you in this alone, Parker?"

Higgins laughed shortly. "He says he doesn't know Harvey Dawson. Well, I do. I met him a couple of times years ago. He's not in Gunsight. We need Parker, Fletch. I figure a party of four is just about right. Not too many, and enough. We'll have to cut straight down to Mexico City and then to Vera Cruz. Four good men can travel fast."

"Four?" Hobbs nodded, thoughtfully. "I catch on."

"You're smart, Fletch. A hundred and fifty bites will eat up most of a cow, but four portions . . . well, you can eat a long time on a fourth of beef. Do you follow all this, Parker?"

"Oh, yes! The boys do the dirty work and we grab the boodle and run. Ha-ha!"

"You think it's funny?"

"Isn't it?"

"A million and a half dollars isn't funny. Nor is one-fourth of that."

"No," said Parker, "I guess it isn't."

A Mexican boy of sixteen or seventeen padded into the saloon and reeled off a few excited sentences. Manuel Higgins slapped the bar with his open palm.

"This is it, men!"

Parker heard a couple of horses trot up outside, then the sounds of men dismounting and hitching their horses. He lined up along the bar with the others, facing the door.

Two men came in. The foremost wore a black broadcloth suit, black stetson and polished boots, into which were tucked his trousers. The second man wore the ragged garb of a Mexican *peon*, down to the *serape* folded and draped over his left shoulder and the immense sombrero, which almost concealed his face. He was an exceedingly swarthy, mustachioed man.

He also wore crossed cartridge belts

and a revolver in each holster. No one paid any attention to him.

"Señor Gallegos!" exclaimed Manuel Higgins. "This is a pleasure."

"The pleasure is mine," replied the representative of the Captain-General of Cuba. He spoke English, but the words dripped with heavy accent.

"Your best whiskey!" Higgins cried.

Everyone turned to the bar, and in turning Parker got a glimpse of the Mexican's face. He did a double take, jerking back for a second glance. The swarthy Mexican tried to duck his face, but saw that he was too late and winked.

The strength seemed to flow out of Parker's body, leaving his muscles like water. For the man, into whose face he was looking, despite the ragged *peon* clothing, the sombrero, the *mustachios* and the deep stain on his face, was Harvey Dawson of Missouri.

16

TOWARD evening, Dick Pendleton rode out to the Layton ranch. He found Jill Layton just in from a ride on the range. She wore a yellow pongee blouse, a divided riding skirt and a sturdy pair of boots. She was hot and flushed and Pendleton thought her the most beautiful girl he had ever known. But Jill was irritated and her greeting lacked its usual warmth.

"Something wrong here?" Pendleton asked.

"Is anything right?"

"No," Pendleton admitted. "I thought for a while today things might improve, but I was over optimistic. Jim Smith is back in town and Johnny Shade shot out the windows of *The Target* office."

"When did Smith get back?"

"This morning. He spent most of the afternoon with Manuel Higgins and finally rode off with him. You know what that means."

"No, I don't. What does it mean?"

"That he's thrown in with Higgins. Well, I'm not surprised. There's a rumor around town that Smith's name isn't Smith. I wouldn't have believed it if it hadn't been for the Higgins business, but after seeing that . . . they say Jim Smith is really the notorious Jim Parker, of Harvey Dawson's gang."

Jill Layton gasped. "Who says that?"

Pendleton shrugged. "The rumor started with a stranger. A man who calls himself Captain Purdy."

"Captain Purdy? What – what does he look like?"

"Eh? Do you know him, Jill?"

"No, I'm just curious. Is he a big, heavy-set man, about forty or forty-two?"

"Why, yes. You *do* know him, then?"

"I saw him – I mean he was pointed out when I was up in Dodge City, with Dad. He's some sort of a policeman, or was."

"I wouldn't be a bit surprised. He's been asking questions all around town. Mmm, he didn't act like he was after Jim Parker – if Smith *is* Parker."

"What if he is Parker? He tried to be a good law officer, the short time they would allow him."

Pendleton laughed. "Jill! You sound queer, defending an outlaw."

"You don't know if he's an outlaw."

"No, but just the same, you've got to admit that he's pretty handy with guns. And his name – why, they say Manuel Higgins has twenty men in his band named Smith."

Jill Layton frowned. "You say Higgins was in Gunsight today? I didn't know that he went around so openly."

"Why not? The streets of Gunsight are full of outlaws and wanted men. Gunsight is the outlaw capital. The Tucson paper printed a piece to that effect a couple of days ago. And it's true. But it won't always be. In fact, it may not last as long as some people think. There's a movement started . . ."

"What movement, Dick?"

"I didn't mean to mention it, Jill. It's still in its infant stages. A number of the more substantial citizens, the mine owners, some of the merchants . . . well, they've been talking about taking the law into their own hands."

"A vigilante committee?"

Pendleton winced. "That's a rather harsh name. I don't think these men would like it. They intend to clean up Gunsight in a legal manner. There's an election coming up in a few weeks, the first in this county. This committee – group, rather – is going to put up a full slate of candidates, of whose honesty there can be no question. They're going to vote for judges, a sheriff, a mayor of Gunsight . . . everything right down the line. And then they're going to clean up Gunsight Valley."

"If they win the elections, you mean."

"They'll win all right, Jill. Every honest citizen will vote for the slate. I'm going to do my very best to see that they do, since I'm slated to be the candidate for mayor."

"Why, that's splendid, Dick!" Jill whirled as she heard the door of the house open. "Mother, Dick's going to be mayor of Gunsight!"

Pendleton reddened. "That may be a little premature. There's talk of putting me up as a candidate in the coming elections."

"You'll make a good mayor, Dick," said Jennie Layton.

"It's not a job I'd want under ordinary circumstances. But I believe Gunsight has a future. The mines seem inexhaustible and Gunsight will become an important city. I intend to remain here and if I have to become mayor in order to do my part toward making Gunsight a decent town, why, then I guess I'll have to do it."

"That sounds almost like a speech, Dick," Jill said, smiling.

"As a matter of fact it is — part of my acceptance speech when I'm nominated," Pendleton chuckled, then almost instantly he frowned. The reason for the frown was the appearance of three horsemen who had come into view on the easy grade approaching the house. They were the two Spences and the evil-looking man known as Dave Temple.

"I see we have company," Mrs. Layton said, drily.

The Spences came up and dismounted. "Evening, Jennie," said Andrew Spence. Then he gave Pendleton a hard look and a short nod. "Like to talk to you, Jennie," he continued. "Something important."

"Very well, Andrew," said Mrs. Layton. "Won't you come into the house?"

They went in, leaving the younger people outside. Kearney Spence looked pointedly at Pendleton. "Were you leaving?"

"No," Pendleton retorted, "I just came."

"Good," said Kearney Spence, "that gives me the chance to ask you some questions. You're from the East, aren't you?"

"Yes, why?"

"Because I was figuring on taking a trip East in a little while." He looked steadily at Jill. "Of course I wasn't figuring on traveling alone, but with somebody else it might be fun . . . if you've got a pile of money to spend and I expect to have it."

"That will be very interesting, Kearney," Jill said. "I hope you'll write and tell all about the trip."

"I'm not much of a hand for writing. Anyway," Kearney cleared his throat, "maybe, you'll be traveling in the East yourself, about that time."

"No," said Jill, "I'm not planning to do any traveling for a long time."

It was a pointed reply to a thinly veiled proposition and Kearney Spence did not seem very happy about it.

In the house, meanwhile, Andrew Spence was more blunt.

"Jennie," he said, "you've got to give me an answer. I've lost two thousand head of stock and I can't put up with it another day."

"I don't understand," Jennie Layton replied. "Arch Cummings tells me we've lost five hundred head ourselves. Surely, you're not intimating that we are rustling your cattle."

"Of course not, but the biggest mistake was to split up our ranch. Don't you see? If it was one, we could protect it, but if your ranch isn't defended you expose my entire east Bank and make me vulnerable to attack. I might just as well have no defense at all as to be exposed in such a manner."

Jennie Layton shook her head in bewilderment. "I don't understand that. Certainly, we are trying to protect our stock."

"With what?" cried Spence. "You've got a dozen riders to protect a quarter million acres. You haven't got enough men to ride one-quarter of your land."

"But that isn't because I don't want to hire men," Jennie Layton said, with warmth. "Arch Cummings has offered ten and fifteen dollars a month above the regular wages and can't get men."

"I've got men," Spence cut in. "I've got enough men to defend this entire valley; good, fighting men."

Mrs. Layton's color had heightened.

"You mean you're proposing again that we merge our ranches?"

"I'm not proposing it. I'm demanding it."

"Demanding?"

"Yes, Jennie, demanding. I've had enough shilly-shallying. Either you listen to reason or I'll take matters into my own hands."

"And what do you call listening to reason?"

"You know very well what I mean. Kearney wants to marry your daughter and I think they should do so at once."

"*You* think so? Well, Andrew Spence, Jill will marry the man she loves and I'm quite sure she doesn't love Kearney."

"What's that?" Andrew Spence cried, angrily. "You're defying me?"

"If you want to call it that."

Andrew Spence's beard seemed to bristle. "You're not in a position to defy me, Jennie. Let me make clear to you — absolutely clear — what will happen if you persist in your folly. My property is being threatened and I won't let *anyone* do that to me. Not even you, Jennie Layton, even though you are the widow of my partner of many years. You act stubborn and I warn you, I'll brush you aside, like I would any man."

Jennie Layton was coldly composed. The only sign of agitation was her slightly flaring nostrils. "I think you'd better go, Andrew Spence."

He strode to the door. "I'll go now. I'll give you twenty four hours — "

"I don't need them. My answer will still be the same."

Spence jerked open the door and stepped out to the veranda. "Come, Kearney!" he snarled at his son.

Kearney Spence seemed quite willing to go. He had been getting the worst of his tilt with Jill Layton and Dick Pendleton. Jill watched the men ride away, then turned to Dick: "Will you excuse me a moment, Dick?"

"Of course!"

Jill stepped quickly into the house and closed the door behind her, so Dick Pendleton could not hear. "Mother," she cried, "did you quarrel with Mr. Spence?"

"I asked him to leave."

"I did practically the same thing to Kearney."

"Good. Then we're washed up with them."

"But are we, Mother? Kearney made some veiled threats."

Jennie Layton bit her lower lip. "You may as well know the truth, Jill, since we're partners. Andy Spence made threats, too. He says he'll take this ranch from us by force if you — if we don't comply with his ultimatum."

"That I marry Kearney?"

"I think he'd be willing to forego that demand if I gave him the ranch, or merged it with him, as he calls it."

"But that's ridiculous, Mother. He can't force us to give him the ranch."

"No, but Jill, I'm worried. I never trusted Andy Spence in the old days. He was always up to something with that outlaw chief, Manuel Higgins, and Higgins has a lot of men at his beck."

"But they can't just come and take the ranch!"

"They can take the cattle. As Andy Spence pointed out, we've got hardly more than a dozen riders. Not nearly enough to cover our range."

"But enough to defend the immediate premises. And you know, Arch Cummings has been bringing the herds in gradually for the last two or three weeks. Most of our stock's within two or three miles."

"I'm wondering if that's such a good idea, concentrating them. A large, well-armed force could take the entire herd in a much shorter time than if they had to round it up in small batches from the entire range."

"Perhaps, but surely no such force would dare an open assault. The law would – "

"What law?"

"Sheriff Grigsby couldn't countenance such an open act of lawlessness. Or could he . . . !"

Jill strode to the door and opened it. "Dick!"

Dick Pendleton came in and shot a quick glance at both Laytons. "Something wrong?"

"Yes," said Jill. "The Spences have made some threats and we're afraid they're not idle. To put it briefly, we think Manuel Higgins is going to raid our ranch and drive off every head of stock we own."

Dick Pendleton whistled. "That's a rather large order, don't you think?"

"Higgins has a large band and – " Jill brought up her chin – "and we're convinced that Andrew Spence is in league with Manuel Higgins."

"That I'm willing to believe. I know that the Spences have encouraged lawlessness in Gunsight and it's been my belief that Andy Spence is the real ruler of Gunsight, subsidizing the sheriff as well as the other town and county officials. But this raid you mention – well, that's a pretty large order. They can't just come and grab off ten thousand head of steers. That takes time."

"Not as much as you'd think. Remember,

the Rio Grande is only nine miles from here. If they get them beyond Gunsight Pass, a few men could hold off an army."

Dick Pendleton's forehead creased. "But would Manuel Higgins dare such a thing? And what could he do with ten thousand head of cattle, below the Border? I understand the country is barren; there are no markets . . ."

"Perhaps he'd drive them inland until this blew over, then bring them back . . . and give them to Andrew Spence."

Pendleton shook his head. "The idea sounds fantastic."

"Of course," said Jennie Layton. She sighed heavily. "Andy Spence blew off steam, that's all."

"Perhaps, Mother," said Jill. "But I – I'm afraid. Kearney's attitude . . . so boastful and sure . . . his hints . . . "

"The young squirt needs a whipping," growled Pendleton. "I've a good notion to give it to him."

"No, don't!" Jill cried. "That man Dave

Temple that follows him everywhere is a bloody killer. He'd shoot you."

Pendleton drew a deep breath. "I think it's time I had a real talk with our committee. Perhaps we are making a mistake, waiting until we can elect a set of honest officers for this valley. Perhaps we'd better — "

"Vigilantes? No, Dick!"

He smiled widely. "Of course not — not that! But I think I'll talk to the committee just the same. Perhaps we can bring some pressure to bear on Andrew Spence. I'd better be riding to town, so I can get them this evening. Good night, Mrs. Layton. Jill . . . "

After he had gone, Jill and her mother seated themselves in the pleasant living-room and discussed the situation. After a few minutes, Jill gave a sudden start.

"Someone just peered in through the window!"

"It's me, Jim Smith!" called a cautious voice.

He stood back from the window, a foot or so. Jill crossed the room. "Come around to the door."

"Rather not," he said. "I've got my horse off a little way. Don't want anyone to see me – not even our men."

Jill hesitated, then raised the window suddenly high. Jim Parker stepped through.

"I've got something to tell you," he said.

17

IN Kangaroo City the conspirators were working out the details of their gigantic rustling plot. The man from Cuba was an experienced scoundrel, it developed.

"I cannot taking chances," he said. "The captain-general giving me the money to buy these cattle. I no bringing – poof! I stand by the wall and get the bullet from the rifle. You bringing cattle to Matamoras and I paying you the money."

"That wasn't the deal, *Señor* Gallegos," Higgins protested. "We'll deliver them across the river and that's all."

"No; that three hundred mile from Matamoras. How I getting fifty t'ousand cattle three hundred mile?"

"You can hire a hundred Mexicans at a dollar a day; that'll still leave you enough profit."

Señor Gallegos flashed strong, white

teeth. “I laying card on the table. You stealing these cattle, no?”

“Well,” said Higgins, “practically. That’s why you’re getting them at a bargain.”

“Bargain is good, but no bargain I not getting cattle on boat. You stealing fifty thousand cattle, no? Cattleman get very angry, no? They chasing cattle, maybe across river, no? I hire Mexican and they don’t fighting so good, I losing cattle, no?”

“No,” said Higgins. “I’ll guarantee there won’t be any fight once the stock’s across the river.”

“How you guarantee?”

“I’ve got more than a hundred boys. There’s a pass up here a mile where a dozen men can hold off a thousand for days. I’ll guarantee to deliver the cattle across the river and have my boys hold off any pursuit for, say, three days.”

A light came into the Cuban’s eyes. “Sound good, but you don’t minding if I seeing this place?”

“Come along; I’ll show it to you

right now."

"Good, but first I telling you — I don't having no money with me now, yes?"

Manuel Higgins grinned. "You're safe enough, now. And you've got a bodyguard, haven't you?"

"Tha's right. Pancho, you coming along!"

Harvey Dawson turned away from the bar and shuffled to the door. When the others came out of the saloon, Dawson was astride his horse and edging it back so that he would be closing up the group as they rode toward the pass leading to Gunsight Valley.

Parker maneuvered his mount to fall back alongside of Dawson. Higgins, Gallegos and Hobbs rode thirty feet ahead. Parker leaned toward Dawson.

"Does Gallegos know who you are?"

"No, of course not," chuckled Dawson. "I picked him up in Matamoras and sold him a bill of goods. I'm getting along and I'd like a nice stake to settle down somewhere. How long have you been with Higgins, Jimmy?"

"I'm not with him."

"Eh?"

"Higgins knows who I am, but he doesn't know that I'm actually working for the Layton ranch."

"You on a ranch, Jim?"

"Yes, I'm through."

"You can't be through, Jim. They won't let you. I know, I tried it myself, years ago."

"I'm going to try it, Harvey. Even though Captain Street is in Gunsight."

Dawson exclaimed softly, "That bloodhound! Lord, do I have to kill him?"

"He says the government sent him here to get Manuel Higgins. But he can't because Higgins has operated too cautiously. But now Higgins is overstepping himself."

"This gets more complicated right along. Jim, I've got to talk to you. Where are you staying, at this Layton ranch?"

"No, in Gunsight. The O. K. Saloon."

"I'll find you there. Shh!"

The riders ahead had slowed as they had reached the entrance of Gunsight Pass. There was a pale half-moon overhead which shed sufficient light for them to make out the dark, forbidding passage.

"How long this?" Gallegos asked.

"Half-mile," replied Manuel Higgins. "Want to go in?"

Gallegos shuddered. "No, I taking word."

"Fine, then let's go back."

As the horses were wheeled, Jim Parker reached out and slapped Harvey Dawson on the arm. Then he edged his horse into the pass and, bending low, put it into a trot.

A hundred yards in the pass, he stopped to listen, but heard no sound of pursuit, so guessed that Higgins and Hobbs hadn't noticed his disappearance. Harvey Dawson, alias Pancho, the Mexican gunman, would cover up for Jim Parker. Even though he was on the opposite side. Dawson and Parker had shared too many blankets in the past.

Parker continued through the pass

and, reaching the open valley beyond, put his sorrel into a ground-covering trot. He traveled a half-dozen miles in quick time, as there were almost no cattle on the range, but when he neared the Layton ranch buildings he had to circle a couple of large herds and was challenged once by a cowboy. Instead of responding, Parker rode out of his way.

At length, however, he saw the lights of the Layton house and when within a couple of hundred yards dismounted and tied his horse to a young cottonwood tree. He approached the house cautiously and saw Dick Pendleton ride away. He waited a few minutes, then went to the window, where Jill Layton saw him.

His manner of approach and entry to the house had alarmed Jennie and Jill Layton. The latter was particularly apprehensive.

"Dick Pendleton was here. He claimed you had thrown in with Higgins."

"That's right. I just left Higgins an hour ago. He's down by the river, arranging to sell fifty thousand head of cattle to a thieving representative of the governor of Cuba."

Both of the Layton women gasped. "Where would he get fifty thousand head of stock?" Jennie Layton asked.

"He's arranging for fifteen thousand head in Mexico; the other thirty-five thousand he intends to pick up here in Gunsight Valley. From you and the Spence place –"

"Spence, you say?" Jill Layton cried sharply. "But Spence is backing Manuel Higgins."

"He has been, but Higgins is pulling a grand double-cross. He's going to strip all the cattle from this valley, drive it through Gunsight Pass into Mexico and then keep going, with a million and a half dollars."

"That's fantastic," breathed Mrs. Layton.

Parker shook his head. "You've bunched your herds, Mrs. Layton. A dozen men could get on the north side of them, stampede them, and the cattle would run straight through the pass, to the shores of the Rio Grande, where a few riders could keep them headed across the river. Why did you bunch your herds?"

"It's because of the rustlers. Arch Cummings . . ."

"Fire him, Mrs. Layton."

"Fire Arch?" gasped Jill. "You want *him* fired? Why, Arch took you – "

"That was *you,* Miss Jill?" Parker asked softly.

Jill became suddenly confused. "Arch has always been with us. He taught me to ride."

"But five or ten thousand dollars is a mighty strong temptation."

"I don't believe it!"

Parker sighed. "I just told you how it looks to me. I heard Higgins and *Señor* Gallegos."

"You mean Higgins told you everything, knowing you were a perfect stranger?"

Parker's mouth tightened. "He knew I was Jim Parker. Captain Street is in Gunsight. He's after Higgins."

"And you!"

"Perhaps, although he said the charge against me has been dropped." It was on the tip of Parker's tongue to say that Captain Street was probably here because he had a clue to Harvey Dawson's presence, but Parker could not bring himself to reveal that, not even to Jill Layton and her mother.

He said: "I believe the drive will be started tomorrow night. I'll be in Gunsight."

He turned to the door, but Mrs. Layton spoke. "Jim Parker, which side are you on?"

"I'm not on Higgins' side," he replied and went out. On the veranda he ducked swiftly to the edge of the house and cut back to his horse.

He mounted and rode to Gunsight.

It was eleven o'clock when he reached the boom town, and the night's activities were in full swing. He took his horse to a livery stable, then started back toward the O. K. Saloon. He had to pass Ethel Halsted's restaurant and, seeing her alone behind the counter, went in. He was hungry.

Ethel's eyes lit up when she saw him, then instantly her forehead puckered.

"Hello," she said in the matter-of-fact tone she would have used for any customer.

He seated himself at a stool by the counter. "I see the rumors have reached you."

"You mean they're not true?" There was unconcealed eagerness in her tone.

"I'm Jim Parker, yes," he said and watched the frown come back to her face. "And I'm from Missouri."

"I didn't want to believe it," Ethel said. "Yet it answered some questions that were in my mind . . . the deadly streak in you. You got that from Harvey Dawson."

"I was eight years old when Order No.11 was issued," Parker said slowly. "My mother watched the Union soldiers burn our house and took me from Clay County to Nebraska. She died there and it was months before my father found me."

Pain crossed her face. "You've never known a happy day; when you grew up you rode with Harvey Dawson. Oh, I know from the papers what you went through. I'm not blaming you, only I wish it hadn't all happened to you. And this Captain Purdy who's here – "

"Captain Street of the Bligh Detective Agency."

"He came here to get you?"

"Perhaps, but he won't. Have you seen Johnny Shade?"

She winced. "He was here an hour ago. You're not – "

"I just wanted to know where he is."

"He's drunk. Jim, please don't – "

He exhaled wearily. "Things are rushing to a showdown. Tomorrow . . . "

"Jim," Ethel Halsted said in a low tone. "Yes, Jim Parker, why don't you leave Gunsight?"

"I can't."

"Damn that bitter streak in you!" cried Ethel. "Damn, why does a man have to fight when everything in him is crying for peace?"

He looked at her, amazed. This was the first time anyone had ever seen through his shell. He said, softly: "Don't you ever want to quit sometimes?"

"I want to quit now," she said, a catch in her throat. "I want to quit and run so fast that it hurts. And I will, if you say the word."

"I can't," he said miserably and getting up, walked out of the restaurant without eating.

Across the street the batwing doors of the O. K. Saloon ballooned outward and a bouncer shoved a man out into the street. He plunged to the ground, rolled over and got up. He started drunkenly down the street.

Parker walked slowly across the street and entered the saloon. He looked around for Matt Royce to ask if his room was still available and his eyes caught sight of a trio at a nearby table. The men were Sheriff Grigsby, stupid-faced Mayor Wiley and a man who was obviously part Indian. There was a badge on his vest.

Grigsby called to Parker. "Jim Smith,

like you to meet our new marshal. Marshal Pelkey, this is Jim Smith who had your job once."

Pelkey did not offer to shake hands. "Yeah, I heard about you. In fact, I heard about you today. Captain Purdy . . . "

"Damn Captain Purdy!" Parker snapped. He turned abruptly away from the table and collided with Kearney Spence who was weaving unsteadily toward the bar.

"Look where you're going!" Kearney Spence snarled. Then he recognized Jim Parker and almost choked. "Uh, didn't see you, Smith. Sorry."

"Smith?" said Dave Temple, coming up behind Kearney. "You don't have to apologize to Smith, Kearney. He bumped you on purpose. I saw him do it."

Parker did something, then, that he had learned from Harvey Dawson long ago. Dave Temple was going to work up a fight with him. When he got to the proper pitch he would go into action and have the advantage.

Parker didn't wait. He took the

initiative before Temple was expecting it. He grinned frostily at Temple, made a half-turn and whipped out his Frontier Model.

Before Temple was even set to draw, the gun in Parker's hand lashed out and struck the gunfighter along the jaw. He cried out hoarsely and crashed backward to the floor. His fingers got his gun halfway out of its holster, then unconsciousness overtook him and he went limp.

Parker started to holster his gun, when something hard was jammed into his spine. "Drop it!" snarled a harsh voice.

There was nothing for Parker to do but obey. A booted foot reached around and kicked the gun to one side. Then the pressure in his back was released and Marshal Pelkey stepped around in front of him.

"I saw it," he said. "Come along with me."

"What?"

"To the calaboose, Jim Smith."

"What for?"

"Cut it out. You think you can go around buffaloing people and not get arrested? What kind of a town do you think this is?"

Parker shot a look past Pelkey at Sheriff Grigsby and Mayor Wiley. The two men were studiously avoiding his glance.

"All right," he said. "Lets go to this jail."

Pelkey retrieved Parker's gun and stuck it in his waistband. His own gun he kept trained on Parker. He fell in behind Parker and they went out of the O. K. Saloon and started toward the calaboose.

Gunsight had modernized its jail. They had a jailer and a couple of prisoners, unshaven miners, from the looks of them.

"This is an important one, Lester," Marshal Pelkey said to the jailer, a grizzled man in his fifties. "Keep a sharp eye on him. And lock your door on the inside after I go out."

Parker went into the cell room and Lester, the jailer, locked the door.

18

JUDGE ANDERSON came into the combination jail and courtroom shortly after eight o'clock in the morning. He brought with him an entourage consisting of Sheriff Grigsby, Marshal Pelkey, Mayor Wiley and Dick Pendleton.

Anderson seated himself importantly behind the table in the corner of the court-room section. "Bring out the prisoners!"

Pendleton came up as Parker stepped out of the cell room. "It's all right," he said, in a low tone. "They won't dare – "

"Silence in the court-room!" thundered Judge Anderson. "First case!"

Sheriff Grigsby said: "Beak Lumley, drunk and disorderly conduct!"

"Twenty-five dollars," Judge Anderson snapped. "Next!"

"Max Helfinger, riding his horse into

the Oro Grande Saloon and shooting at the lamps."

"Twenty-five dollars. Next case!"

"Jim Smith, assault with a deadly weapon."

"Ah," said Judge Anderson, leaning forward. "Jim Smith, a former marshal of this town. A man who *knows* the law and can't plead ignorance. What have you to say for yourself, Smith?"

"Would it be any use?"

"What's that? Why, you insolent pup, that's one hundred dollars fine for contempt of court. Now, how do you plead on the assault charge?"

"Well," said Parker, "you fine murderers twenty-five dollars, so – "

"Jim!" exclaimed Dick Pendleton. "Don't . . ."

"I warned you before to keep quiet, Pendleton," Judge Anderson said, grimly. "Now, go ahead, Smith, I fined a man twenty-five dollars for what?"

"For cold-blooded murder . . ."

"Wait a minute!" cried Manuel Higgins, coming into the court-room. "I want to pay this man's fine."

Parker, watching, saw Judge Anderson's eyes shoot to Sheriff Grigsby's face. The latter nodded.

"Your fine's one hundred dollars," the judge said. "I'll pass up that contempt of court stuff . . ."

"Here's the money, Judge," said Manuel Higgins tossing five double eagles to the table. "Come on, Jim."

Parker was tempted to refuse Higgins' payment of the fine, but knew that it wouldn't solve things. He shrugged and fell in beside the outlaw chieftain. They left the court-room and descended the flight of stairs.

At the bottom, Fletch Hobbs and Johnny Shade fell in. Johnny Shade was glowering, but Fletch Hobbs smiled. "Missed you last night, Jim. Get lost in the dark?"

"Something like that. Well boys, I'll see you later . . ."

"Why not now, Jim?" Manuel Higgins asked. "You've had a good night's rest and I thought we might take a little ride."

Parker's gun had not been returned to him. Three of the deadliest men in the Southwest flanked him. They would almost as soon shoot him here on the street as somewhere else.

Parker said, "My horse is at the livery stable."

"That's where our'n are."

Leaning against the hitch-rail in front of the O. K. Saloon was Captain Street. He chuckled. "Morning, Mr. Higgins, Mr. Smith, Mr. Shade and Mr. Hobbs. What I wouldn't give for a good camera!"

"You . . . " began Johnny Shade, but Higgins cut him off.

"Shut up, Johnny. Like us to come and sit for a picture some day, Captain?"

"I sure would. Up north I could get rich, selling prints."

"Oh, I thought maybe you wanted the picture for Colonel Bligh."

"Naw, that wouldn't be necessary, on account of the colonel's coming here. Yep, I'm waiting for him right now. He's on the morning stage."

"Well! that *is* a surprise. Sorry, I can't

wait for the stage Captain Street – "

"Purdy – just like Jim Parker's name is Smith, you know."

"Yeah, sure. Well, Captain Purdy, would you tell the colonel for me that if he waits around I'll be in to see him tomorrow? Just like to talk over old times."

"I'll do that little thing, Mr. Higgins. Tomorrow, eh?"

"Tomorrow!"

They continued down the street, crossing to go to the livery stable. Inside, the liveryman had the horses ready and saddled, including Parker's. Higgins had been sure Parker would return with him. Parker made a mental note of that.

As they rode out of the stable, Parker caught a glimpse of Dick Pendleton in front of *The Target* office. He was talking to a heavy-set man who wore a frock coat.

The quartette of horsemen, three armed and one unarmed, rode westward out of town. After they cleared Gunsight, they turned south down Gunsight Valley.

Then Higgins spoke to Parker. "Why'd you run out last night, Parker?"

"Because the setup is crazy. You can't swing it."

"Is that the only reason? You didn't run off because you wanted to tip off the Laytons?"

"What do you think, Higgins?"

"You slapped down Dave Temple."

"He's been gunning for me ever since I arrested his charge, Kearney Spence, weeks ago. He was going to draw on me and I beat him to it."

"Then why didn't you kill him?"

"The setup wasn't right. Grigsby and Pelkey were there. You saw what Anderson was going to do to me this morning?"

"What?"

"He was going to keep me in that calaboose."

"Ah, stop it," snarled Johnny Shade. "You know he's lying, Higgins."

"Fletch," said Parker, "lend me a gun."

"Sorry, I'm out of bullets."

"I've got two guns," Johnny Shade volunteered. "We'll settle this once – "

"Johnny!" cried Higgins. "And you, Fletch. I warned you about Shade yesterday."

"Keep your trap shut, Johnny," growled Fletch Hobbs.

Johnny Shade sniffed, but subsided. Higgins rode in silence for a moment, then resumed, "This is a big game, Parker. You heard too much yesterday. That's why I've got to be careful. And I *can* swing it. You'll find that out. I'd put a lot of stock in you yesterday and then you let me down."

"You're serious, Higgins? You think you can rustle fifty thousand head of cattle and get away with it?"

"You'll see, Parker. You'll see, because you'll be riding with us. From now until this time tomorrow you'll be right close to one or the other of us at all times. We just can't take any chances of anyone talking to the wrong people."

19

JILL LAYTON spent a restless night. She had virtually denounced Jim Parker, yet his words remained with her and created a doubt that would not be stilled. She was up with the dawn and when the first cowboy appeared out of the bunkhouses, she was crossing the ranchyard.

"Arch!" she called.

Arch Cummings came out of the bunkhouse, shivering in the morning chill. "Yes, Miss Jill."

"I want to talk to you. You have practically all of our cattle within a few miles of the ranch."

"That's right; we haven't got enough hands and we can look after them better if they're bunched."

"Yes, but supposing a large force of rustlers descends, wouldn't it be possible for them to run off the entire herd down through Gunsight Pass?"

The foreman looked at her in astonishment. "Who'd tackle a herd the size of our'n?"

"Manuel Higgins!"

"Shucks, he wouldn't dare."

"Suppose he would?"

"That's out of the question."

"Perhaps, but we can't take even the slightest chance. I think you should disperse the herd."

Arch Cummings' face darkened. "If your mother gives the order. She's the boss."

It was a direct rebuff to Jill and she turned and went to the house, where her mother was just having breakfast. She told of the interview with Cummings.

"Will you give him the order, Mother?"

"I was going to before you told me. You see, I somehow believe that Jim Parker, the outlaw, is an honest man. He's a tragic figure, a man who had no youth, who got off to a wrong start and can't fight back . . . unless someone lets him make the fight."

Jill Layton's cheeks were hot. "Jim Parker's a killer. I can never forget that. I've tried to, but I can't. After I learned that Kearney Spence killed a man, I've shuddered every time I've seen him. And I *saw* Parker kill a man, that stage robber. Parker wasn't even angry when he drew the derringer and shot the robber."

"But wasn't he doing it to protect you?" Mrs. Layton asked, quietly.

Jill had no answer for that. She went out and had one of the hands saddle her horse. Mounting, she rode over the crest south of the ranch house. A shallow basin covering two or three miles was a solid mass of cattle. In the distance she saw Gunsight Pass.

Start the herd south, stampede it . . . and there was only one way it would go. Ten thousand head of cattle would pour through Gunsight Pass, across the shallow Rio Grande into Mexico.

Although she searched the fringes of the herd, she saw no more than three riders, far, far too few for this job. She turned her horse and rode back to the ranch.

Her mother met her at the veranda and, before Jill could dismount, said, "Arch quit!"

"Because you told him to disperse the herd?"

"Yes, although he said something about there being too many bosses . . ."

Jill exclaimed angrily, "Then Parker was right. Arch had been bought."

"I'm afraid so, Jill. And I've checked, we have exactly fourteen hands on our payroll. Three are on the range now; I've asked the rest to wait for an announcement I want to make to them. I wanted you to hear it."

Mrs. Layton walked out to the center of the area between the ranch house and the bunkhouses. The cowboys who had been loafing around came to a semblance of attention. There were eleven, for Arch Cummings had already left.

"Men," Mrs. Layton said, "most of you have been on the Layton ranch for years. You know what we went through to build up this place and you know that the Laytons don't give up anything without a fight. Well, we're faced with that right now. I have reason to believe that an effort will be made by rustlers to drive off our entire herd. I expect every man who remains here to defend this ranch and all that is on it, but I'm willing to pay off any man right now who is not willing to fight. To those who are, let me say that there will be a bonus and a job here as long as the Layton ranch is in existence."

A bandy-legged cowboy stepped forward. "I'm a cowhand, Miz Layton. I'll do any kinda work, but I don't figure on no gunplay. I'd like my wages."

"Very well, you shall have them — and good luck to you. Is there anyone else?"

The men shuffled around, looking at one another, but finally two additional men asked for their time. At that one of the loyal cowboys said, "And I hope you buy poisoned whiskey with the money you draw!"

There remained eight loyal hands, not counting the three on the range. Eleven at most. Manuel Higgins had ten times that many, all accustomed to horse and revolver work.

Jill Layton's face was as gray as ashes. "I'm going to Gunsight, Mother," she said. "I'm going to ask Jim Parker to come here, if I have to beg him."

"You won't have to do that, Jill," said Jennie Layton soberly. "But you know the worst now. If we're to survive, we've got to fight . . . "

"I can marry Kearney Spence."

"Do you want to marry him?"

"No, but we can't lose everything for which you and Father worked so hard – "

"Then let's fight!"

Jill Layton rode to Gunsight as fast as her horse could take her; too fast, for if she had gone slower, she would have seen, only two miles from the ranch house, a group of four horsemen riding a half-mile west of the road. Jim Parker was one of the group.

But in her speed, she did not see the riders and so she rode to Gunsight, dismounting in front of the office of *The Gunsight Target.*

Dick Pendleton turned from a type case as Jill entered.

"Jill!" he cried. "I was just thinking about you."

"Thanks, Dick," Jill said crisply. "I came to town to find Jim Parker. Can you tell me . . ."

"He rode out a half hour ago; with Manuel Higgins, Fletch Hobbs and Johnny Shade. Higgins paid his fine — "

"Fine?"

"Oh, you don't know. It seems Parker assaulted young Spence's bodyguard, a blackguard named Temple. He was arrested and kept in jail overnight. This morning Judge Anderson fined him a hundred dollars."

"Jim Parker was brawling?"

Pendleton shrugged. "I didn't see it. But the talk's that he provoked the fight. He struck Temple with the barrel of his revolver."

"And they arrested him for that? Kearney Spence murdered a man and was fined only twenty-five dollars."

"Spence is on the right side. But why this sudden interest in Jim Parker?"

"I want to offer him the job of foreman of our ranch. Arch Cummings sold us out. Mother and I believe an attempt will be made to run off our entire herd of cattle tonight."

"But that's absurd, Jill!"

"We don't think so," Jill replied stiffly.

"But Parker, he's in with Higgins. Higgins paid his fine."

"I know; but what you don't know is that I employed Parker in Tucson to come back to Gunsight."

Pendleton blinked. "You did *that?*"

"I did. And he said he intended to throw in with the outlaw gang and get an inkling of their plans. He did and told us last night. The plan was so stunning we didn't believe him, and then . . . he came to Gunsight."

Dick Pendleton whistled. "I wonder. I was at the courtroom this morning and for a moment I got the impression that Parker didn't want to go off with

Higgins and the others, that they were actually threatening him."

"They were! He must have run off from them yesterday and they followed him to Gunsight. His life's in danger. They may already . . ."

"They may," Pendleton admitted soberly. "If this had only held off a few days. The committee . . ."

"The committee!" Jill exclaimed scornfully. "They'll hold meetings and then they'll go home and lock their doors on the insides."

Pendleton flushed. "The committee decided last night not to wait until the elections are held. They decided to ask for the resignations of Sheriff Grigsby, Mayor Wiley, Judge Anderson and all the other political tools of Andrew Spence."

"And suppose they refuse to resign?"

"Then they'll force them."

"But Judge Anderson and the sheriff are appointees of the territorial Governor."

"That still doesn't change their characters. Jill, I'd like for you to go across the street with me to Detterback's store. Detterback is with me in this and I'd like you to tell him what you've told me."

"Very well, Dick."

Detterback's store was a large one-story place where everything was sold from needles and thread to mining machinery. There were a half-dozen clerks in the store, but Dick Pendleton led Jill to a small office in the rear, where Detterback was going over an account book. He was a man in his early forties, large and very muscular. He had a black, spade-shaped beard that was six inches' long.

Jill was acquainted with him through having made purchases at the store, and the storekeeper greeted her with profuse warmth. Pendleton cut him off.

"Miss Layton has something to tell you, Detterback."

Quickly, Jill told of the rustling threat. Detterback listened, nodding now and then, but when Jill finished he shrugged. "You told Miss Layton about the committee, Pendleton?"

"Of course. And the reason I brought Miss Layton here is to urge the committee to act now instead of waiting."

"But our plan was to clean up the town of Gunsight, not the county. After all, we can't — "

"You can't!" Jill snapped. "But you built your town on our land. This ground on which your store is built — from whom did you buy it? To whom are you paying rent?"

Detterback winced. "That lawyer fellow, Kennard, has been harping about that for weeks. I guess there's no question about who the land belongs to, and one of these days, we're going to have to pay you rent. I expect to pay when the rest of them do."

"And what are you going to do — drive the outlaws out of Gunsight into the valley?" Jill went on. "Will they stay there? Or will they kill and rob in the town and then hide in the valley?"

Detterback tugged at his beard while his dark eyes glowed. Then he reached for his coat. "Go home, Miss Layton. Things will be taken care of. Today."

Pendleton's face was taut. "This is the time, Detterback. Jill, I'll ride out before evening, or send word."

The two men strode out of the store, with Jill following a few paces behind. She started to cross the street to where her horse was tied, when Ethel Halsted came out of her restaurant and called to her.

"Miss Layton!"

Jill turned. "Yes?"

"I'm Ethel Halsted. I – I run this restaurant."

"I know; I've seen you."

"And I've seen you. At the dance when Jim Par – Smith was shot. It's about him I want to talk."

"What? You know him?"

"He eats at the restaurant. He's – oh, you must have heard the rumors about him, his real identity."

"He's Jim Parker of Missouri; is that what you mean?"

"I do. It's that I want to talk to you

about. He passed here this morning with Manuel Higgins, Fletch Hobbs and Johnny Shade. I know Johnny. He's bad, a killer. He was in the restaurant earlier and boasted that he was going to get Parker. He dropped something about they'd found him out and – "

Jill Layton stiffened. "Manuel Higgins said that to Shade?"

"Yes, I gathered it was Higgins who had found out that Parker had learned their plans and was going to reveal them. They took him out of Gunsight to kill him; I'm sure of that, but I don't know what to do about it, how to stop them. There isn't anyone in Gunsight I can trust and I knew – mean, I've seen Jim looking at you . . . at the dance . . . and I thought . . . "

"I came to town this morning to offer Jim Parker the job of foreman of our ranch. We're in dire peril out there and we need him. Miss Halsted – Ethel – what you've just told me verifies what I was beginning to suspect, that Parker is in immediate danger. I – I think I know where they'll be taking him. I'll get my men to rescue him."

Jill had not been through Gunsight Pass since her return from the north. She knew that outlaws hid along the river, that they used Gunsight Pass to come and go, but she did not know about Kangaroo City.

But she raced across the street and swiftly mounted her horse. She waved to the worried-looking Ethel Halsted, then put her horse into a gallop.

A half-mile out of town she overtook a Mexican astride a huge black horse. He was a swarthy, ragged individual, but wore two well oiled revolvers. Jill swung out to pass the Mexican, but he called to her and sent his horse after her.

Jill, looking over her shoulder, saw the big horse gaining on her own mount and kicked it in the belly with her heels. The horse seemed to flatten and gave the race everything he had, but inside of two minutes, the Mexican had drawn up beside Jill. A swarthy hand lunged out and caught the bridle of Jill's mount. He pulled the horse to a halt.

Then he smiled widely. "You are Mees Layton, no?"

"Let go of my horse!" Jill cried, more angry than frightened.

"Sure," the Mexican replied. "I don't wanting steal. I got better horse now. You, Mees Layton, I talking to you, *si?*"

"What do you want; a job? All right, I'll give you one."

"Working job?" The Mexican shuddered. "Pancho don't like working job. I want asking you 'bout Jeem, what you call Jeem Smith?"

"You know him?"

"Si, good frien'."

"I'm looking for him!" Jill cried. "He left Gunsight this morning, headed this way. He was with some men who intend to kill him. I've got to find him!"

"Heegeens?"

"Higgins, yes. You know – "

"I knowing," said Harvey Dawson, still posing as a Mexican. "How long they going this way?"

"An hour, maybe longer."

"Goo'bye!" cried Dawson. He suddenly let go of the bridle and his big black leaped forward.

Jill put her own horse into a gallop, but the black of Dawson's increased the distance so quickly between them that inside of a mile, Dawson was a quarter of a mile ahead.

20

THE population of Kangaroo City had swelled since the day before, for Manuel Higgins had sent out the word. Twenty-five or thirty horses were tied at various places and the saloon was crowded with villainous-looking men, the scum and fugitives of two countries.

They hailed Higgins with a roar as he entered the saloon, accompanied by Fletch Hobbs, Johnny Shade and Jim Parker.

"What's the job, Manny?" they cried.

"You'll find out tonight," Higgins shouted. "But you can bet it's a big job that'll give you enough money to have all the fun you want."

"Will there be enough money to take a trip and buy me a set of store teeth?" asked a toothless outlaw.

"There'll be enough to buy a set for

every day of the week and a solid gold one for Sundays," Higgins retorted.

He pushed through the saloon into a small room in the rear, which was just large enough for a table and several chairs.

"I've got a few things to look after," Higgins said to the others. "Take me a few hours. I want you to promise me, Fletch, that you'll stick right here – and not to let Johnny get drunk."

"I don't need a wet nurse," Johnny Shade sneered.

"The devil you don't," Higgins snapped. "I'm holding you responsible, Fletch. And Parker, I wouldn't try anything if I were you." He nodded significantly to Hobbs.

Parker pushed a chair out of the way and stretched out on the floor. "I didn't sleep well last night. If you don't mind – " He closed his eyes.

Higgins went out and Hobbs and Shade seated themselves at the table. "How about a game?" Fletch Hobbs asked.

"Two handed?"

"We can get a couple of the fellas in the other room. Just a minute." Hobbs left the room.

Johnny Shade promptly walked around to where Parker lay on the floor and kicked his boot. "I hear you been shining up to Ethel Halsted."

Parker opened his eyes and looked up at Shade. "Quiet, Johnny, I want to sleep."

Shade kicked viciously at Parker's boot. "Damn you, Parker!"

Parker drew his feet under him and rose. "If you still want to lend me that gun, Johnny . . . "

Fletch Hobbs opened the door. "Hey, Johnny, for the love of Mike, can't I turn my back on you one minute?"

Shade swore and, pulling out a chair, sat down at the table. "Did you get any players?"

"They're all broke. There isn't five dollars in the crowd. Pickings have been slim. Higgins is giving them credit for the drinks."

"I'll sit in a hand," said Parker. "Unless you'd rather just rob me of the money I've got."

"Cut it out, Parker," growled Hobbs. *"I* haven't got anything against you. Neither has Manny; he's just being cautious and you can't blame him, the kind of job this is going to be."

Parker sat down at the table. He brought out a fistful of money. "What will it be — table stakes?"

"Suits me. You, Johnny?"

"All right."

Fletch began shuffling the cards he had obtained in the other room, but before he could deal, the door was pushed open and Harvey Dawson came in.

"Ah!" he exclaimed. "You are playing the poker?"

"Hello, Pancho," said Fletch. *"Señor* Gallegos here?"

"No, but he coming later. Where *Señor* Heegeens?"

"He isn't here. You wouldn't have any money on you, would you, Pancho?"

"For playing the poker? Ha! I am one

best poker player in all Mexico. Look!" He reached into a pocket and brought out a handful of gleaming gold pieces.

"Sit down!" cried Johnny Shade. "Sit down and show us some of that Mexican poker."

There were more than twenty double eagles and several smaller gold pieces in Dawson's pile.

"*Señor* Gallegos must pay you well," Fletch Hobbs remarked.

"*Si,* and am I not the best revolver shot in all Mexico?"

Fletch winked at Johnny Shade. "Kinda modest, ain't he?"

"*Si,*" smiled Dawson. "Now, how you playing this poker? No limit?"

"That's right – just like in Mexico."

Fletch Hobbs dealt five cards all around. Parker, who was on Fletch's left, got a pair of kings and opened for five dollars. Johnny Shade was next and called. Then Dawson tossed in a twenty-dollar gold piece. "I don't like change, raising, I take the plunge."

Fletch Hobbs whistled. "You play

them steep, eh, Pancho?" He looked at his cards, frowned, then put twenty dollars into the pot.

Parker kept an ace for a kicker and drew two cards. One of them was an ace, giving him two pairs, ace high. Shade drew two cards. Dawson then threw four cards into the discard. "I keeping ace. Maybe I catch two more, hey?"

Fletch Hobbs swore. "And you raised on that?"

"I am very lucky."

"You must be, to be the best poker player in all Mexico," Shade said sarcastically.

"Be that as it may," Parker said, "I bet twenty dollars."

Shade scowled. "And you only drew two?" He shot a quick look at Dawson, who was holding his cards close to his chest and smiling broadly. Shade threw in his hand. "Beats my pair of queens."

"I catching," said Dawson, so I'm raising fifty dollars."

"Jeez!" cried Hobbs. He threw his hand in angrily.

"I call your fifty," said Parker, "and I raise you back a hundred."

"Ha! You are bluffing, *si?*"

"No, I'm not bluffing."

"Then I calling." Dawson spread out his hand. "I catching one ace, so I am making pair. Is good, no?"

"Is good, no," said Parker and showed his hand.

Dawson exclaimed in chagrin, "Ah, you are ver' lucky!" He had lost a hundred and forty dollars on a single hand.

It was Parker's turn to deal. He got a complete bust and stayed out while Hobbs and Shade whipsawed Dawson for two hundred dollars, the pot finally going to Johnny Shade.

All but fifty dollars of Dawson's money went on the third deal which Shade won again. And then it was Dawson's deal. He shuffled the cards clumsily and when Johnny Shade cut them he spilled half of the deck and had to shuffle over again. Finally he dealt.

Parker looked at his hand and held his

breath for a moment. He knew what had happened, because he knew that Pancho was actually Harvey Dawson . . . and Dawson was one of the best sleight-of-hand artists in the Middle West.

Parker's hand consisted of four queens and an ace.

Yet on his right, Fletch Hobbs was squinting closely at his hand. And Johnny Shade was trying very hard to look bland.

Hobbs said, "I've got to win a hand sometime. I open for twenty dollars."

Parker merely called, guessing that Hobbs would be raised anyway. He was, by Johnny Shade. Fifty dollars.

"Ha!" cried Dawson. "Everybody got good hand, maybe I winning back what I lose." He shoved in his fifty dollars, then searched his pockets and brought out five more double eagles. He put one into the pot.

Fletch shook his head. "I'll play these. I like 'em."

Parker discarded his ace, for the effect, and drew a ten in its place. Johnny

Shade drew one card and Dawson three. Fletch winked at Johnny Shade when he saw that.

"I bet a hundred," Fletch said.

Parker called and Johnny Shade, counting out money, hesitated and finally raise a hundred. That brought it up to Dawson, who was short a hundred and twenty dollars. He searched his pockets once more and fished up a lone twenty-dollar piece. He groaned heavily and took off his boot. "Is bad luck not calling all bet," he said and brought out four double eagles from the boot. "Am still short twenty dollar."

"You can call for that much," Fletch said, "if you think you're still lucky."

"Am lucky, but not breaking luck. Here – " he drew one of his well oiled Frontier Models – "I got two. One good for twenty dollar, no?" He beamed at first Fletch, then Shade.

"Good by me," said Fletch. He fanned his hand, then looked at the money in front of Parker. "You playing table stakes, Parker?"

All of Parker's money but thirty-five dollars was in the pot. He nodded without expression.

"Good," said Fletch. "Then I raise Johnny and you thirty-five dollars."

Johnny called and exclaimed peevishly, "Best hand I've had tonight and nobody's got any more money. I've got four jacks."

"Sacramento!" cried Dawson. "I am ruin. I got only pair ten. I make bluff."

Hobbs slammed the table with his fists. "And with that you bucked my ace-high full house?"

"And my four queens," Parker said quietly.

"What?" cried both Fletch and Shade.

Parker dropped the cards on the table and reached for the pot. His right hand fell carelessly on Dawson's revolver and he used the muzzle to help rake in the money.

The eyes of both Shade and Fletcher were on the big Frontier Model. They were Parker's guards . . . and he had acquired a gun under their very noses.

"Give him back the gun," Fletch Hobbs said, tautly. Parker smiled. "I won it, fairly – and it's a good gun."

"Is dam fine gun!" boomed Dawson. "But watching trigger, very fine. I buying him back from you sometime, no?"

"Sometime, yes."

"Put it down, Parker," Johnny Shade whined. "Put it down, or – "

"Or what?"

"You know what I mean." Both of Johnny Shade's hands were at the edge of the table.

"Don't, Johnny," Fletch Hobbs said.

And then Johnny Shade went for his gun. He was lightning fast and even in the somewhat awkward position, drawing from his linen coat pockets, his draw was a remarkable one. But Jim Parker had a gun in his hand. He tried to give Johnny Shade a fair break and waited until Johnny's hand was coming up, but then he merely flipped the gun to the side and fired.

Johnny cried out, half rose from his chair, then went over backwards.

Parker flicked the gun to the right and caught Fletch Hobbs with his hand on his gunbutt.

"Go ahead, Fletch," he said softly.

Slowly, Fletch brought up his hand. "Not this time, Parker . . . but Johnny was my pardner. He had maggots in his brain, but he was my pardner just the same."

"Madre mio," whispered Harvey Dawson. "What is happening in here?"

Somebody banged on the door from in the saloon and a rough voice called: "Anybody hurt?"

Fletch got up and opened the door. Parker stepped behind him. "Private argument," Fletch said shortly and closed the door again.

"I'll be going, now," Parker said then.

"All right, Parker, but I'll be seeing you."

"Tonight?"

"Tonight, if you're there."

"I'll be there. Tell Higgins." He stepped to the door. "I could kill you now, Fletch."

Fletch shook his head. "I won't draw – now. So you couldn't kill me. That's your handicap."

"Maybe it is," said Parker, nodding thoughtfully. "And yours, too. What about the Mex?"

"Me?" said Dawson, rolling his eyes. "Is one big mistake. Why you fighting?"

Fletch looked bitterly at Dawson. "Because you're the stupidest hombre in all Mexico."

Parker stuck Dawson's revolver into the waistband of his levis and opened the door. He walked swiftly through the saloon and outside found his horse. The number of horses had increased since he had entered less than an hour ago. The outlaws obviously were still coming in.

Gunsight Pass was clear, but at the northern edge, Jim Parker encountered a half-dozen heavily armed men. One of the men held up his hand.

"We're Layton cowboys, Parker. We came to get you, but there were too many down at Kangaroo City. We're mighty glad to see you."

"Miss Layton sent you?" Parker asked in astonishment.

"Yep. Arch Cummings quit his morning and the boss said you were the new foreman. That's all right by us, but there are only twelve of us altogether. We don't like the looks of that crowd on the other side of Gunsight Pass."

"I don't either," Parker said crisply. "They're going to raid tonight. The first thing we'd better do is break up the Layton herd. Scatter it as widely as possible, to make it more difficult for them. If we had only twenty-five or thirty men, I'd be for half of them standing them off right here and the others — no, that wouldn't work, because Higgins might make a deal with Spence and then double-cross him, like he's planning on doing now."

"Spence isn't in with Higgins?" one of the cowboys asked.

"Spence thinks he is. But Higgins is taking his herd, too. But we're only working for the Layton Ranch. We haven't much of a chance against Higgins' gang of cutthroats, but we'll make it as hard for them as we can."

"How's he going to get rid of that many stolen cows?" another cowboy wanted to know.

"That's a long story," Parker told him. "It'll have to wait till we get a few cows scattered. Come on, boys, let's get busy!"

21

GUNSIGHT had seen a lot of excitement in its short life, but it was to see something new today. It began before nine in the morning, but developed so gradually that it was some time before the town at large became aware that anything out of the ordinary was taking place.

Here and there a man came out on the street and walked to Detterback's big store. He went in but did not come out again. Not for a half hour or more, when the front door of the store was opened and heavily armed men began pouring forth. There were almost two score. They moved in a solid body up the street until they came to the mayor's office, which was in an adobe shack next door to Wells Fargo.

Here the crowd stopped, with the exception of the leaders, Dick Pendleton,

Louis Detterback and Eli Bishop, the leading blacksmith of Gunsight.

Mayor Wiley, in undershirt and trousers, got up from a cot in the rear of his office. "Morning, gentlemen!" he greeted the trio.

Detterback jerked his left thumb over his shoulder. "Take a look outside, mayor."

Wiley blinked, then peered past Detterback through the dirty windowpane. He gasped. "What's – what're all them men outside for?"

"They came to ask for your resignation as mayor of Gunsight."

Mayor Wiley's bleary eyes threatened to pop from his head. "I – I never wanted to be mayor in the first place."

"Then you'll resign?"

"Yes – yes, of course. I resign right now."

"Write it out, Wiley. But first a note discharging Pelkey as marshall of Gunsight."

"Of course, anything you say, gentlemen!"

Wiley seated himself at a table and

scribbled feverishly. When he finished he handed two sheets of paper to Detterback. His hand was trembling.

"Thank you, Mr. Wiley," Detterback said. "Now, just a suggestion which might be beneficial to your health. Why don't you take a trip, say to Tucson, or maybe even to California?"

"An excellent idea," Wiley said, licking his lips. "I think I'll leave at once."

The leaders of the citizens' group left Wiley's shack in time to meet Marshal Pelkey forcing his way into the crowd.

"Break it up!" Marshal Pelkey cried. "What's going on here?"

Detterback thrust a piece of paper at Pelkey. "You're fired, Pelkey. Here's the mayor's order."

The half-breed's face darkened. "What the hell you tryin' to pull? Wiley can't fire me!"

"But he did," said Dick Pendleton. He plucked the nickle-plated badge from Pelkey's vest. "Sue the city for your back wages."

Pelkey made a move for his gun, but

Eli Bishop caught his wrist in an iron grip. Detterback took his gun away. "If you're wise, Pelkey, you'll start moving and keep right on going out of Gunsight. Come on, men, we'll go have a talk with the sheriff."

But Sheriff Grigsby had already seen them coming. He stepped out of the combination court-room and jail and rested a double-barreled shotgun on the railing. A slight pivot would bring it facing the stairs.

He called down, "Anything I can do for you, gentlemen?"

"Your resignation," Detterback replied.

Grigsby shook his head. "Sorry, the governor gave me this job. He's the only one who can ask me to resign."

"*We're* asking you to resign," Dick Pendleton cried. "Mayor Wiley has discharged the marshal and handed us his own resignation."

"That's too bad," Grigsby said, grimly, "but I can't resign."

"You've got to, Hal Grigsby," yelled Eli Bishop. "We mean business."

Grigsby pivoted the shotgun so that it pointed down at the men below. Bishop, Detterback and Pendleton were in the front rank and they would catch the full blast of the gun. So would some of the other men, for at the distance – some twenty feet – the gun would scatter.

"I mean business, too," Grigsby said. "You'll get me, but some of you won't know about that."

Those below knew that the sheriff meant his words. He was in league with the ruffian element, no doubt of that, but he was a courageous man. Yet for the committee to back down at this stage meant their complete defeat. Already several of the men behind the leaders were grumbling.

Dick Pendleton leaped into the breach. "We don't want any unnecessary bloodshed, Grigsby. We'll make a deal with you . . ."

"No deal," Detterback said, doggedly.

"Listen," Pendleton insisted. "Grigsby, you won't resign, but you can assume an inactive status for a while. Appoint one of us a deputy and he'll assume your duties."

"You, Pendleton? Will you wear the deputy's badge?"

"Yes, if no one else wants it. We've got a job to perform and it will be much better if it has a semblance of legality."

"All right," conceded Grigsby. He lowered the muzzle of the shotgun . . . and it was the last thing he ever did. Somewhere in the crowd a gun exploded and Grigsby jerked back. He stood for a moment, feet wide apart, staring down in amazement. Then his body crumpled and bounced down the entire staircase, landing at the feet of Detterback and Pendleton.

A couple of the committee members brought forth a white-faced youth who worked in one of the stores. "I — I thought he was going to shoot," the youth babbled.

"Get away from here," Louis Detterback said in disgust. "Get away from here and ride out of Gunsight."

"Yes, sir," the youth said and started running.

Pendleton shook his head. "Grigsby *was* still sheriff. This won't sound good at the capital."

"What's done is done," said Eli Bishop. "Who's next?"

"Judge Anderson!"

They found Judge Anderson at the bar of the O. K. Saloon. In the same place they found young Kearney Spence playing cards with a couple of professional gamblers. The citizens' committee rounded them all up, but dealt with Judge Anderson first of all.

"We want you to write out your resignation as judge," Detterback told Anderson, "then we want you to telegraph it to the governor."

"This is insurrection," blustered Judge Anderson, "an armed uprising against the duly appointed officers of the United States government."

"Uh-huh," said Detterback, "but they did the same thing up in Virginia City, Montana, when things got too bad . . . and one of the Vigilantes is now a United States senator."

"Vigilantes!" gasped Judge Anderson. "You wouldn't . . ."

"Sheriff Grigsby died five minutes ago," Eli Bishop said, although he did not add how the sheriff had died. It was enough for Judge Anderson. He seized the paper and pen that Matt Royce brought him and wrote out his resignation, addressing it to the territorial governor.

Dick Pendleton handed it to one of the men. "Rush this to the telegraph office. The minute it's on the wire, we'll call it official and Judge Killian will be the only judge in this county. So I guess we might as well start giving Spence that trial for which he's been overdue."

"No!" yelled Kearney Spence, hoarsely. "No, no!"

But every member of the citizens' committee had been reminded by Dick Pendleton's words that Kearney Spence, in addition to being a blustering hellion, had murdered the one-time marshal,

Plennert, in cold blood.

"Get Judge Killian!" the cry went up.

The judge came into the saloon within three minutes. When the situation was explained to him, he hesitated. "This isn't the way to do it."

"It's the only way," Louis Detterback insisted. "Gunsight's had enough of the other way; crooked politicians protecting murderers and cutthroats. You're supposed to be an honest judge, Killian. All right, pick your jurors. We'll round up the prosecuting attorney and we'll let Spence have an attorney – anyone in town he wants. What do you want that's more legal than that?"

Judge Killian nodded. "That's better, with the prosecuting attorney handling the prosecution and a defense attorney for the defendant . . . as long as he gets a fair trial!"

The trial of Kearney Spence began ten minutes later. The prosecuting attorney belonged definitely to the Anderson-Wiley-Grigsby faction. Though he was unnerved by the events of the morning, he plunged into the task of prosecuting Kearney Spence with considerable if somewhat forced vigor.

Spence had babbled for an attorney named Needham, but when the latter appeared, red-eyed with an evident hangover, Spence changed his mind and begged for Attorney Kennard, who was considered the most upright advocate of the law in Gunsight.

Kennard accepted and did his best, but the result was a foregone conclusion. There were no less than a dozen men in the citizens' committee who had been present in the O. K. Saloon on the evening, weeks ago, when Kearney Spence had taunted Marshal Plennert and then killed him. Attorney Kennard made a plea for leniency, but the jury, with less than five minutes' deliberation in a back room, came out and announced a verdict of guilty and recommended hanging.

Judge Killian became a little white at that, but pronounced the sentence.

Kearney Spence broke down completely.

He fell to his knees and begged for his life. "Please!" he sobbed. "Don't kill me now. Give me time; until tomorrow. My father . . . "

"How much time did you give Marshal Plennert?" Dick Pendleton asked harshly, although he too was taut and pale.

"String him up now!" someone cried. "He'll never be any guiltier."

None who were present at the trial knew that Dave Temple had ducked out of the back door of the O. K. Saloon when the committee came in by the front. They did not know that Temple had mounted his horse and put it into a dead run all the way to the Spence ranch.

Even while the jury was deliberating the fate of Kearney Spence, his father, at the head of thirty hard-riding, fighting men, was thundering down upon Gunsight. And behind them riders were quickly rounding up the rest of the Spence hands, who at the time were out on the range. They had orders to drop everything and come in groups or singly at top speed, to Gunsight, to earn the fighting wages they had been drawing for two months.

The citizens' committee brought Kearney Spence out to the street. A block away, to the west, a two-story frame building was in the process of construction. A six-inch joist that was to hold the roof projected out two feet. It was about fifteen feet from the ground.

Kearney Spence was carried here, for his legs had turned to rubber so that he could not walk. A carpenter's horse was set under the joist, but for a moment Kearney was not to step on it.

Captain Street and a barrel-chested man with iron-gray hair suddenly stepped out of the crowd, and the former knocked over the carpenter's horse. The barrel-chested man threw up his hands.

"You can't do this, men!" he roared in a tremendous voice. "I won't let you. I'm a deputy United States marshal and I command you to disperse."

"You're a what?" Dick Pendleton challenged.

"I am Colonel Bligh of the Bligh Detective Agency, and I hold a special United States marshal's commission."

Pendleton sneered. "Yesterday your associate was hobnobbing with the biggest outlaw in this country, Manuel Higgins. He was on friendly terms with Jim Parker."

"He was acting under orders," Colonel Bligh retorted. "He had a warrant for Jim Parker's arrest, but knowing the situation here, he was sure he couldn't serve it."

"That's just it, mister," snapped Louis Detterback. "That's a situation we're remedying now. We had enough of lawlessness. This man here was tried by a jury, in a court presided over by Judge Killian, an appointee of the Territorial Governor. We're merely carrying out the sentence. And if you, mister, will arrest this Manuel Higgins or any other outlaw, we'll give them the same fair trial. Until then, move over!"

Far up the street, a volley of gunfire broke out. The citizens' committee, turning in a body, saw a large body of horsemen approaching at a gallop.

"Look out!" someone cried. "It's Andy Spence and his killers . . . "

The citizens' committee suddenly began to mill, but Louis Detterback's powerful voice roared above the din. "Stand steady, men! There aren't enough of them to lick us . . . Steady and if they shoot at us, give them hell!"

The approaching cowboys were already slackening the speed of their horses, and a hundred yards away they deployed across the street and came to a halt. Andy Spence came on alone.

"What have you done to my son?" he cried when he was still some distance away.

"Dad!" screamed Kearney Spence. "They're going to hang me!"

"Kearney! Come here!"

Kearney tried to break through the men surrounding him, but they would not permit it. Kearney bleated. "Dad, they won't let me . . . "

"I'll count ten!" roared Andy Spence. "You let Kearney go or I order my men to open fire . . . and there'll be fifty more men here inside of a few minutes."

"Now, wait a minute, Spence!" exclaimed Detterback. "We don't want a war here, but your son was tried for the murder of Marshal Plennert and found guilty."

"I don't give a damn what you found, you're not harming my boy. Now, let him go, because I'm starting to count. One . . . two . . ."

A couple of the men closest to Kearney Spence gave way and Kearney suddenly broke through the crowd. "Dad!" he cried.

Dick Pendleton whipped out his revolver and fired at Kearney. Kearney Spence screamed, stumbled and plunged forward a few feet, falling to his face less than ten feet from his father's horse.

Andrew Spence started to dismount from his horse, but a sheet of flame and roll of thunder from his riders behind caused his horse to rear and throw him to the ground. He landed heavily, but got to his knees and began firing at the citizens' committee, which was dispersing in a mad frenzy.

Spence's riders charged forward, shooting furiously at the scurrying citizens.

But they had not counted on one thing: that the committee was the voice of the majority of the citizens of Gunsight. Although not active members they had known what was going on in Gunsight for the past hour. They had taken positions all along the street and were watching all the proceedings. They saw Andrew Spence and his riders coming into Gunsight and they knew that trouble was coming. So while Spence was issuing his ultimatum, scores of Gunsight residents were lining up by the windows of stores and business establishments. And all were armed.

As the cowboys charged the citizens' committee, gunfire broke out from the stores and, inside of thirty seconds, the street was the scene of a bloody slaughter. Horses and riders went down, cowboys began scurrying about as wildly as had the committee a moment before. Horses screamed and men yelled hoarsely. And above it all rose the staccato rattle of gunfire.

Less than half of Andrew Spence's men got clear of the battle scene and they met the main force of Spence riders coming into Gunsight. They numbered close to sixty men with their reinforcements. But they did not risk a charge down the street.

22

DICK PENDLETON, publisher of *The Gunsight Target,* a non-fighting man, had fired the shot that started the battle on the street of Gunsight. And in the holocaust that followed he dashed unscathed into Ethel Halsted's restaurant.

Ethel, frightened, was just going into the kitchen, where her Chinese cook was cowering by the stove. Dick Pendleton leaped after Ethel and caught her in the kitchen.

He gripped her arm so savagely she screamed. "Let me go, you murderer."

"What do you mean? Where are you going?" Pendleton cried hoarsely.

"I saw what you did outside and I know what you are. I've known for a long time. Johnny Shade hinted at it."

Out on the street the fight was raging; at any moment someone might burst into the restaurant to take refuge. There would be many casualties in Gunsight. Even an innocent bystander might be shot.

Dick Pendleton said, "You won't get to tell that outlaw friend of yours. I was afraid that drunken Shade would blab. So . . ."

He brought up his gun. The Chinese cook, who had been standing by, suddenly screamed and whipping up a meat cleaver, threw it at Dick Pendleton. Pendleton ducked frantically and the lethal weapon sailed over his head, crashing into some pots and pans beyond. Pendleton thrust out his gun, pulled the trigger and the Chinese went over backwards, moaning.

Ethel Halsted was just sprinting through the back door. "Damn you!" cried Dick Pendleton. He sent a bullet after Ethel, then lunged after her.

The dying Chinese, with almost his last breath, rolled over and clawed at Pendleton's ankle, upsetting him.

Outside, Ethel Halsted heard another shot back in her kitchen. It gave her heels additional speed. She ran a hundred feet, then darted into the back door of Detterback's General Store. There were a half-dozen men in it, crouching down below the level of the front windows through which they were shooting out upon the street.

Ethel ran to a side door, plunged through and went into the back door of Mueller's Photograph Gallery. By the time she got through this, the gunfire had abated and she risked going out to the street.

A quick glance showed her that Spence's cowboys had retreated westward up the street. Ethel ran to the hitch-rail, picked out a big black gelding and, loosening the slip knot that tied him to the post, struggled into the saddle.

The stirrups were much too long and she was not a good rider, but she didn't care. She turned the gelding's head toward the east, slapped it on the flank, then held on for dear life.

The black gelding Ethel Halsted had commandeered was a splendid horse and covered the ground with amazing speed. Before she realized it, Ethel had cleared the town of Gunsight and had to turn the gelding's head to the south, so she could circle back and get on the main road that led to the Layton ranch.

She did not know it, but actually she was traveling a two-mile circle, that Dick Pendleton, by cutting straight south of Gunsight, traversed in less than a mile.

Ethel, on the galloping gelding, was stunned to see Dick Pendleton, on a big roan, waiting beside the trail.

Pendleton threw up his hand which contained a revolver. Sobbing, Ethel leaned low over the gelding's neck and kicked it in the belly with her heels. The animal increased its speed and rushed past Dick Pendleton.

Ethel didn't hear the report of Pendleton's gun, but suddenly the world seemed to stop for her. Pain that wiped out everything enveloped her. Instinctively her arms clawed the gelding's mane and she retained the saddle, but for several minutes Ethel was not aware of anything at all.

Excruciating pain finally made her gasp, and she sucked in a great lungful of air and became aware of life. She discovered that she was still riding and that the animal under her was running as she had not believed it possible for anything to run. And every step jolted Ethel.

She bit her lower lip with her teeth until blood flecked her chin . . . and still she clung to the saddle.

She did not know if Dick Pendleton were pursuing her; she did not care. She stayed on the gelding because it was the only thing she could do. She did not have strength enough to halt the horse, or even to let go and throw herself sidewards to the ground.

She just hung on and the gelding covered ground. And then after a while the pain became less acute and finally went away altogether. She raised her head then and saw the ranch buildings of the Layton ranch ahead.

The gelding's speed slackened, partly

from exhaustion, partly because it recognized a ranchyard ahead after five miles of open range and believed this to be its destination.

Before the veranda of the Layton house the horse came to a heaving stop. Jill Layton, hearing the hoof-beats, came to the window, then jerked open the door and sprang out.

"Ethel!" she cried. Then, as she saw the blood that had stained Ethel Halsted's shirtwaist, "Oh, my dear!"

Mrs. Layton came running and, with Jill's aid, lifted Ethel from the saddle. But Ethel groaned and they laid her on the ground. The wounded girl's eyelids fluttered and her lips parted in a faint smile.

"I came to warn you," she gasped. "All the Spence cowboys are in Gunsight, fighting the Vigilantes . . . a pitched battle. It's a plot!" A grimace of pain wrenched Ethel's face and for a moment she could not speak.

When she tried, Jill Layton sobbed, "Please don't . . . you're hurt!"

"I know, but I've got to talk. Dick Pendleton started it all. He's – "

"Dick Pendleton, you say?" cried Jill. "Oh, you must be mistaken."

"No; Johnny Shade told me . . . Pendleton is Higgins' younger brother. He's working with Higgins; his job was to draw all of Spence's men out of the valley, so Higgins could raid, so . . . "

South of the Layton ranch house, gunfire broke out. Ethel Halsted groaned. "Too late. Jim Parker could have stopped it. I – you've got to warn Parker. Captain Street and Colonel Bligh are in Gunsight. They want – " Ethel Halsted suddenly choked and coughed. Blood bubbled up from her lips.

Her eyes blinked and then became staring . . .

A horrible sob wracked Jill Layton and her mother's strong arms went around her, and helped her to her feet. "She's the bravest girl we've ever known," she said, simply.

"She came to warn us," cried Jill. "She came because of Jim. And Dick . . . "

Dick Pendleton brought his horse up in a cloud of dust and bounced to the ground. He shot a quick glance at the body of Ethel Halsted, then strode toward the Laytons. His gun was still in his hand and his face was different from the way Jennie or Jill Layton had ever seen it.

He knew from their expressions that Ethel Halsted had talked.

"Get on that horse, Jill," he said, harshly. "You're coming with me."

Jill shrunk away from him. "No!"

"Get on that horse," Pendleton repeated. "Get on, or . . . " He whipped up his gun and pointed it at Jennie Layton.

Jill screamed. "No, no!" Then she broke loose from her mother and rushed to the horse Ethel Halsted had ridden.

"Wait, Jill!" cried Mrs. Layton. She turned and ran toward the house.

"Get going," Pendleton ordered. He mounted his own horse again, brought it up beside the big black gelding and caught the reins. "Come on!"

The horses sprang away and were gone

a hundred feet before Mrs. Layton came out of the house with a shotgun. The range was much too far for that gun, Jennie Layton knew. She couldn't hit Pendleton without hitting her daughter.

She stood there in front of her home and watched Pendleton and Jill reach the crest of the hill.

23

TWELVE men to break up a herd of ten thousand cattle; there weren't enough of them to do the job in the short time they had at their disposal, perhaps six or seven hours. Yet they would have made a good start at it had they been allowed that much time. Parker had counted on it. He hadn't thought Higgins would advance into Gunsight Valley before dark.

But he didn't know Higgins' timetable. He didn't know that Higgins had gone out to meet an emissary from Gunsight, who told him that the citizens' committee was going into action, was in action by the time Higgins received the news.

Higgins reached Kangaroo City within a half-hour after Jim Parker had killed Johnny Shade and made good his escape. By that time fifty or sixty outlaws had gathered. Higgins would have preferred waiting for the rest of the gang that swore allegiance to him, but events had forced his hand and he promptly gave the order to Fletch Hobbs.

"Its up to you, Fletch. The Laytons have a dozen riders; the Spences seventy or eighty, but they won't be on the range. You'll find that their herds will be pretty convenient." He chuckled wickedly. "If they're not, I've thrown away a lot of good money. I want to see steers pouring through that pass in an hour, and by evening I want to see a million and a half dollars' worth across the river. D'you understand?"

"Yes," said Fletch Hobbs, "but I've got to get Jim Parker."

"You fool," snarled Higgins, "do you want revenge or one-third of a million dollars and a half?"

"One-third?"

"You and me — and another."

"Who?"

"My brother . . . the man who's handled the Gunsight end of things all along."

"I didn't know you had anyone there."

"You'll meet him tonight. Now, are you going through with this with me or not?"

"A half-million dollars is too much money for anyone to kick in the face. But where are you going to be while all this is going on?"

"Across the river, with *Señor* Gallegos, counting the steers as they come across. I'll be right close to his money."

"You wouldn't try anything Higgins?"

"What do you think?"

"I'll follow you to Mexico City, anywhere."

Higgins laughed. "You won't have to. Get going – Oh you'll have a little help in the valley. Arch Cummings, who used to be foreman of the Layton ranch, will show up with a few boys. You'll know them by the white sheets they'll be flashing to stampede the cattle. Make it easier for you. You can concentrate on the Spence stuff."

"You think of pretty near everything, Manny," said Fletch Hobbs.

"That's why I've lived so long."

And in Gunsight Valley, Jim Parker and his eleven men were riding into the huge Layton herd, breaking out a few hundred head at a time, driving them away from the main bunch and pushing them quickly to the north or east. Usually when they got a few hundred head a halfmile from the big herd, they stampeded them, knowing very well that the animals would run until exhausted. They'd lose some cattle that way, but it was better than losing them all.

In an hour they had dispersed nearly a thousand head, but nine-tenths of the herd was still intact. And so it would remain.

A rider came galloping from the south, waving his hat. "The rustlers are coming!"

And they were!

A long column of them was filing out of Gunsight Pass. As they cleared the walls on either side they broke the file and massed in a solid bunch.

Jim Parker looked at them and said, "Let it go, boys. They're too many."

The cowboys stared at him with

astonishment. "You mean to quit without a fight?"

"What's the use of fighting if you're only going to get killed? They've got us outnumbered five to one. We'll lose the herd anyway and knowing we died won't help the Laytons."

"You yellow . . . " one of the cowboys spat out.

Parker shrugged. He suddenly whirled his horse and headed it eastward. He had gone a quarter of a mile before the first shot was fired. He turned in his saddle, then, to watch the fight.

The outlaws were charging in a solid body. Leaderless, the cowboys broke and fled in every direction. Parker saw only one fall from his saddle before the outlaws turned from the pursuit and headed westward.

Parker nodded in satisfaction. The men thought him yellow, but only one of their number had been lost. Had they fought all would have been exterminated. Even Jim Parker.

And Jim Parker still had work to do.

The cards had been stacked against him in Gunsight Valley. He hadn't had a chance to win, because it had been the other side who had dealt the cards.

But now Jim Parker was going to deal.

He slapped his horse and it broke in to a gallop. After a few minutes he turned its head in an easterly direction, toward the forbidding peaks of Gunsight Range. A horse couldn't scale those cliffs, but a man might. And on the other side was the Rio Grande – and Mexico!

Jim Parker deserted his horse at the foot of the mountain range; three miles west was Gunsight Pass, through which cattle were streaming. Along there were Higgins' men.

But here where Jim Parker started his ascent was only a rugged mountain, rising almost a thousand feet from the floor of the valley.

The first few hundred feet up the mountain were comparatively easy and Parker covered them in short order, but from then on the climbing became more difficult, and he had to weave back and forth seeking a foothold. Soon he was using his hands as well as his feet.

It was around noon when he started his climb and the sun was already low in the west when he finally reached the pinnacle. He threw himself down on the rocky perch and rested for fifteen minutes. Then he got up and looked down at the Rio Grande.

Cattle were pouring across the river and the far side of it was a vast sea of moving flesh.

Parker began his descent of Gunsight Range, which was vastly easier. It took him only a half-hour, and when he finally reached the sandy ground below he kept moving toward the river, without pause.

It was easy enough to cross. It was a dry, hard-baked bed for most of the distance. The water that flowed down was confined to narrow, shallow streams that cut the bed in a few places.

On the Mexican side of the river, Parker paused a moment. The thousands of cattle were making a hideous noise.

The earth rumbled continuously from the steady pounding of their hoofs.

Riders galloped their horses up and down along the fringes of the herd, keeping the stock together, keeping it moving in an easterly direction. From the huge sombreros, Parker guessed that the riders here were Mexicans.

He started walking toward the herd. When he neared it he stopped beside a Joshua palm and waited for a galloping rider to come up. When that happened he stepped out and threw down on the Mexican.

"Pile down from that horse!"

Whether the Mexican understood English, Parker didn't know, but the gun and gesture could be understood in any language. The Mexican climbed down from the saddle. His feet had hardly touched the ground when Parker hit him with the barrel of his gun. As the man slumped to the ground, Parker caught him and swiftly unbuckled the man's cartridge belt. He crossed it over his own.

He removed the *serape* from the dead Mexican and stuck his head through the hole in the center. It draped his figure, concealing most of his clothing. He finished by putting on the man's huge sombrero, which was much too large for him and came down over his ears. Parker had to tilt back his head to see from under it, but with it kept down he doubted if anyone could see his face.

It took him a few minutes to catch the dead man's horse, but he finally effected it and, mounting, galloped toward the west, where the Spence and Layton herds were making their crossing of the Rio Grande. The stream had thinned considerably, he noted, and, looking across the mile stretch of water and sandy bed of the Rio Grande, Parker saw that only a trickle of cattle was coming through Gunsight Pass. That meant the job would soon be over.

24

HE caught sight of a large body of horsemen sitting motionless in the shade of a clump of cottonwoods. As he neared he saw that they were mostly Mexicans.

A little to the right was a smaller group, which consisted of Manuel Higgins . . . Dick Pendleton . . . and Jill Layton. Dick Pendleton was holding the bridle rein of Jill's mount. At the sight of the latter two a ripple ran through Parker. Jill was the last person in the world he had expected to see here. But he had no time for speculations.

Galloping across the river was a clump of riders led by Fletch Hobbs. Arch Cummings and Dave Temple were in the group. As they reached the shore line a man wearing a black serge suit detached himself from the Mexicans and approached Higgins' group.

Parker, who was less than a hundred feet away at the top, heard him cry out: "They are finished!"

"You made your tally?" Higgins replied. "When the rest of these come across, you'll have a bonus of almost five thousand head."

"That is fine," said *Señor* Gallegos. "Then we shall say *adios* until three days?"

"What?" cried Manuel Higgins.

"But you remember the bargain. You said you would hold the pass for three days."

"I said that, but if you're meaning what I think you are, you got another thought coming. A very short one."

"I do not understand?"

"The money; you're shelling it out right now."

"But then I have no guarantee that you will protect the pass!"

"You've got my word!"

"But all this money; it do not belong to me. My captain-general . . . "

"The hell with your captain-general."

During the altercation Hobbs' group had reached that of Manuel Higgins. They made a dozen altogether, but a short distance away were more than that many Mexicans and a few shots would bring many more.

Parker had eased toward the Mexican group. Because of his disguise the Higgins group would think he was one of the Mexican group.

The situation was delicate. *Señor* Gallegos looked at the well-armed Americans and realized that when the bullets started to fly he would probably be the first to stop lead. He shrugged.

"I make the bargain with you, *Señor* Higgins. I give you one half the money now and – "

"You'll give it all, right now. That's the bargain. Fork over or – " Higgins suddenly whipped out a long-barrel Frontier Model and rode up to within six feet of Gallegos.

His act had been seen by the Mexicans, and sunlight flashed on metal in many hands, those of the Mexicans as well as the Americans. It was at this juncture that one of the Mexicans pushed his horse away from the others. Parker, noting it idly, received a sudden shock, for the man was Harvey Dawson.

The representative of the Cuban governor capitulated under the threat of Manuel Higgins' gun.

"Very well, I make the payment now, but you give me your promise to guard the pass for three days?"

"Yes," said Higgins. "I'll make you that promise."

Gallegos called to his men and one of them rode forward carrying a well-filled wheat sack. He dropped it on the ground. Gallegos dismounted and, after he had given another order, a *serape* was spread on the ground.

Higgins and several of his men dismounted and gathered around the blanket. The wheat sack was opened and bundles of greenback currency were dumped out.

Harvey Dawson clucked to his horse and it moved forward. Parker said, softly:

"Harvey!"

Dawson's head pivoted quickly. Parker tilted back his head to reveal his face. Dawson whistled and brought his horse up beside Parker. "Jim, are you in this with me?"

"You're after that money?"

"It's more than I got in all the years of riding and shooting . . . and hiding. I can quit, Jim."

"I'm sorry," Parker replied, "but I quit months ago."

Dawson sighed wearily. "Bligh and Street are across the river. They'll be on your trail – and mine – and they never quit. You know that."

"I know, but I'm not going on . . . after this."

Dawson looked steadily at Parker. "That girl!"

"What girl would have me?" Parker snapped, bitterly. "What girl could be happy with a man who rode with Harvey Dawson?"

Dawson winced. "A girl said that to me once. It must have been a hundred years ago . . . Did you know that that slick bird there with the girl killed another this morning? To keep her from telling about this raid. A girl named Halsted."

"Ethel Halsted! Pendleton *killed* her!"

Parker started forward, but Dawson gripped his arm and held him back. "Wait! I know what's going to happen. Gallegos is going to pull off with his men, as soon's the money is counted. And if I'm not guessing wrong, your friend Higgins is going to get rid of most of his men and then start making tracks with the boodle. That's when I start."

"You're going to hold him up?"

"For a million and a half!"

The count was finished now. Gallegos was mounting his horse and shaking hands with Manuel Higgins. "Good-bye, *Señor!*"

"Happy voyage," Higgins replied sardonically.

Gallegos went back to his *vaqueros.* There was a sharp command, then they were wheeling. Someone called to Harvey Dawson and Parker.

"Come on," Dawson whispered. "We'll be back in a few minutes."

They fell in at the rear of the Mexicans, who went into a trot.

Dawson and Parker kept their horses trailing behind the others and, as the main body went over a low dune, Dawson turned his horse toward the river. Parker followed. They were three or four hundred yards from the Higgins group.

They saw several men detach themselves and start back across the river.

"Now," said Dawson.

Parker kneed his mount and it broke into a trot. As he and Dawson descended upon the Higgins group he saw that it consisted of Manuel Higgins, Dick Pendleton, Jill Layton, Arch Cummings, Fletch Hobbs and Dave Temple.

Higgins saw them coming and snarled: "Get back with your gang, you — "

Parker drew up his horse and dismounted. Dawson followed.

Parker threw off his big, concealing sombrero.

"Parker!" cried Higgins.

An unholy light came to the eyes of Fletch Hobbs. *"Thanks,* Parker."

"Wait a minute!" cried Harvey Dawson.

Higgins gave Dawson a contemptuous glance. "Get going after your boss, Pancho. This doesn't concern you."

"Ah, but it does . . . because my name isn't Pancho." He laughed wickedly. "The mustaches fool you, Higgins? I didn't have them when we met – back in Missouri . . ."

Manuel Higgins took a step forward. He peered into the face of Harvey Dawson, then recoiled as if he had been struck.

"Harvey Dawson!"

"Harvey Dawson!" repeated several throats.

Dick Pendleton's grip fell from the reins of Jill Layton's horse. Jill quickly turned her horse away. Pendleton lunged out again for the bridle rein.

"Let go!" cried Jim Parker.

Dick Pendleton whirled and clawed for his gun. Parker shot him through the body, turned and fired at Fletch

Hobbs. But Hobbs's bullet beat him by the fraction of an inch and lead seared through Parker's left thigh. The leg gave way under him and he fell to the ground, but even as he fell, his left hand brought up the gun that he had taken from the Mexican not so long ago.

He hit the ground on his face, rolled over instantly and came up to a sitting position. By that time Harvey Dawson had killed Manuel Higgins and was throwing down on Arch Cummings.

Fletch Hobbs was trying desperately to hold himself in the saddle. But he was slipping sidewards. He cried out hoarsely, "Damn you, Parker!" and, letting go, hit the ground.

Parker shot him again, deliberately.

Cummings was down now and Dave Temple was in full flight. Dawson, his face bleeding from a wound over his left temple, aimed calmly and dropped Temple from the saddle.

"Here they come!" he cried, exultantly.

On the ground, Parker turned and saw the group of Higgins' men, who had left a few minutes ago, start back. There were at least ten or more.

Jill Layton sprang from her horse and fell to her knees beside Jim Parker.

"Jim, get up! We've got to ride."

"You ride, Jill!" Parker said, "I'll hold them off."

Harvey Dawson stepped over Parker and, reaching down, caught him under both armpits. He jerked him up roughly. "Get on your horse, Jim. That's an order!"

"Yes, yes!" Jill babbled. She caught a horse herself and brought it up to Parker, helped put his foot into the stirrup. As Parker swung up, Dawson turned to Jill. "And you, too! Take that damn sack of money and get going." He scooped it up and tossed it to the saddle in front of Parker.

"Harvey," said Parker, looking down at his one-time chief.

"What the hell would I do with a million dollars?" Dawson snarled.

The advancing riders had reached the shore line three hundred yards away. Too far for accurate revolver shooting. But in a moment . . .

"Ride!" roared Harvey Dawson.

"Harvey!" yelled Parker.

"You fool," Dawson raged, "do you want that girl to get shot? Ride; I can hold them all back . . . long enough."

For just a second longer Parker hesitated. Then he choked and nodded to Jill Layton who was already astride a horse.

The first shot was fired by the advancing riders as Parker slapped his horse.

A hundred yards away, Jim Parker looked over his shoulder. Harvey Dawson was lying prone on the ground, firing at a wildly gyrating mass of men and horses. Two or three men were already down.

Later, Jim Parker said to Jill Layton, "He wanted it that way. I guess he figured it made up some . . . "

Jill Layton nodded soberly. "He did it for you, Jim. He did it because of what he had done to you . . . And now, Jim?"

"You'll get your herd back. The

Mexican government will never permit that many stolen cattle to be shipped out of the country. You can return this money to the Cuban governor . . ."

"Yes, but that wasn't what I meant, Jim Parker. I said, what about you?"

"Me? Why, I'll be riding."

"Where? Haven't you been everywhere?"

"I've been everywhere I want to go. But . . . *Jill!*"

And then she was in his arms and Jim Parker knew that he would ride no more.

Other titles in the
Linford Western Library:

TOP HAND
Wade Everett

The Broken T was big. But no ranch is big enough to let a man hide from himself.

GUN WOLVES OF LOBO BASIN
Lee Floren

The Feud was a blood debt. When Smoke Talbot found the outlaws who gunned down his folks he aimed to nail their hide to the barn door.

SHOTGUN SHARKEY
Marshall Grover

The westbound coach carrying the indomitable Larry and Stretch headed for a shooting showdown.

FIGHTING RAMROD
Charles N. Heckelmann

Most men would have cut their losses, but Frazer counted the bullets in his guns and said he'd soak the range in blood before he'd give up another inch of what was his.

LONE GUN
Eric Allen

Smoke Blackbird had been away too long. The Lequires had seized the Blackbird farm, forcing the Indians and settlers off, and no one seemed willing to fight! He had to fight alone.

THE THIRD RIDER
Barry Cord

Mel Rawlins wasn't going to let anything stand in his way. His father was murdered, his two brothers gone. Now Mel rode for vengeance.

ARIZONA DRIFTERS
W. C. Tuttle

When drifting Dutton and Lonnie Steelman decide to become partners they find that they have a common enemy in the formidable Thurston brothers.

TOMBSTONE
Matt Braun

Wells Fargo paid Luke Starbuck to outgun the silver-thieving stagecoach gang at Tombstone. Before long Luke can see the only thing bearing fruit in this eldorado will be the gallows tree.

HIGH BORDER RIDERS
Lee Floren

Buckshot McKee and Tortilla Joe cut the trail of a border tough who was running Mexican beef into Texas. They stopped the smuggler in his tracks.

BRETT RANDALL, GAMBLER
E. B. Mann

Larry Day had the choice of running away from the law or of assuming a dead man's place. No matter what he decided he was bound to end up dead.

THE GUNSHARP
William R. Cox

The Eggerleys weren't very smart. They trained their sights on Will Carney and Arizona's biggest blood bath began.

THE DEPUTY OF SAN RIANO
Lawrence A. Keating and Al. P. Nelson

When a man fell dead from his horse, Ed Grant was spotted riding away from the scene. The deputy sheriff rode out after him and came up against everything from gunfire to dynamite.

FARGO: MASSACRE RIVER
John Benteen

The ambushers up ahead had now blocked the road. Fargo's convoy was a jumble, a perfect target for the insurgents' weapons!

SUNDANCE: DEATH IN THE LAVA
John Benteen

The Modoc's captured the wagon train and its cargo of gold. But now the halfbreed they called Sundance was going after it . . .

HARSH RECKONING
Phil Ketchum

Five years of keeping himself alive in a brutal prison had made Brand tough and careless about who he gunned down . . .

FARGO: PANAMA GOLD
John Benteen

With foreign money behind him, Buckner was going to destroy the Panama Canal before it could be completed. Fargo's job was to stop Buckner.

FARGO: THE SHARPSHOOTERS
John Benteen

The Canfield clan, thirty strong were raising hell in Texas. Fargo was tough enough to hold his own against the whole clan.

PISTOL LAW
Paul Evan Lehman

Lance Jones came back to Mustang for just one thing — revenge! Revenge on the people who had him thrown in jail.